"Come with me, Betty, just a moment. We have some business to discuss," Max said, propelling her into the hallway.

He pulled her so quickly her flowing silk skirt threatened to become trapped between her legs. They stopped in a softly lit corner, and he faced her, the intensity in his eyes filling her with a mixture of dread and excitement.

"A moment," she whispered with a note of warning. She felt herself swaying toward him. "What did you want to discuss?"

"Just this—if you want to be kissed in public, come to me." He put his arms around her waist and pulled her up so that she had to grasp his shoulders for support.

"Max. Max . . ." she said desperately, shaking her head.

"I love your voice. Say my name again."

"Maximilian, don't—"

He kissed her, backing her against a soft quilt hanging on the wall. Betty struggled with her emotions for the length of time his hot, deliciously insistent mouth took to turn her into a conspirator. About two seconds.

She forgave herself for surrendering. He had a way of curling the tip of his tongue along the edge of her upper lip that no woman could resist. He brought a rough power to her that she'd never felt before. He didn't treat her roughly in the least, but she wanted to struggle within his arms and provoke the same struggle from him. He had trapped her, but he wasn't forcing her. . . .

WHAT ARE *LOVESWEPT* ROMANCES?

They are stories of true romance and touching emotion. We believe those two very important ingredients are constants in our highly sensual and very believable stories in the *LOVESWEPT* line. Our goal is to give you, the reader, stories of consistently high quality that may sometimes make you laugh, sometimes make you cry, but are always fresh and creative and contain many delightful surprises within their pages.

Most romance fans read an enormous number of books. Those they truly love, they keep. Others may be traded with friends and soon forgotten. We hope that each *LOVESWEPT* romance will be a treasure—a "keeper." We will always try to publish

LOVE STORIES YOU'LL NEVER FORGET
BY AUTHORS YOU'LL ALWAYS REMEMBER

The Editors

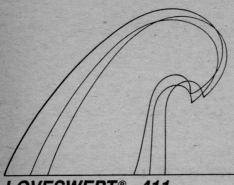

LOVESWEPT® • 411

Deborah Smith
Honey and Smoke

 BANTAM BOOKS
NEW YORK • TORONTO • LONDON • SYDNEY • AUCKLAND

HONEY AND SMOKE

A Bantam Book / July 1990

*LOVESWEPT® and the wave device are registered
trademarks of Bantam Books, a division of
Bantam Doubleday Dell Publishing Group, Inc.
Registered in U.S. Patent
and Trademark Office and elsewhere.*

*If you would be interested in receiving protective vinyl
covers for your Loveswept books, please write to this address
for information:*

*Loveswept
Bantam Books
P.O. Box 985
Hicksville, NY 11802*

ISBN 0-553-44041-1

Published simultaneously in the United States and Canada

*Bantam Books are published by Bantam Books, a division
of Bantam Doubleday Dell Publishing Group, Inc. Its trademark, consisting of the words "Bantam Books" and the
portrayal of a rooster, is Registered in U.S. Patent and
Trademark Office and in other countries. Marca Registrada.
Bantam Books, 666 Fifth Avenue, New York, New York 10103.*

PRINTED IN THE UNITED STATES OF AMERICA

OPM   0 9 8 7 6 5 4 3 2 1

For my cousin, Rita, who knows her barbecue. For my pal, Laura, who knows her marines and for my husband, Hank, who knows the secret recipe.

One

As a way to recapture his youth it was lousy. As a belated homecoming ritual it stank. It couldn't erase the twenty years spent away from these north Georgia mountains, twenty years served with great pride in a marine uniform. It couldn't bring the old spirit of excitement to his blood again or make the autumn air smell like an invitation to adventure, as it had when he was a kid.

All it could do was stand there majestically in a grove of sourwood trees, silhouetted against the burnished red leaves, its large dark eyes peaceful and unsuspecting. All it could do was make Max Templeton realize in the space of a few seconds just how much he had changed in twenty years. And that he had killed enough in his life. He wasn't interested in killing again, not even a deer.

He felt foolish and perplexed, not unusual emotions for him in the six months since his retirement from the Marine Corps, but painful nonetheless. He had retired to see if there was something new to be learned about himself, but he wasn't sure that he liked what he'd discovered.

So now he convinced himself that he was going to do what he would have done twenty years ago, or even five

1

years ago. And would have done without a qualm. He was going to shoot the deer. He remained crouched in the gully, the powerful hunting rifle butted expertly against his shoulder, his large hands holding it without effort, his thick, callused forefinger posed lightly on the trigger. Seconds ticked by. He didn't shoot. He began to curse silently.

He muttered to himself. "Did you hear about Major Templeton? Big, tough son of a gun. A twenty-year man, and not even forty yet. Real career grunt. He thought he could retire and live like a civilian again. Yeah, it broke him. Now he's in a home, drooling in his oatmeal. Keeps saying, 'Bambi, Bambi, Bambi.' "

Max squinted down the rifle's sight. *Leave, dammit,* he told the buck silently. *And I'll just pretend I'm posting for a picture in* Field and Stream.

The buck didn't depart, but something else arrived. Something that bounced out of the underbrush and vaulted over the gully. Something furry that thumped Max in the back of the head as it sailed past.

Max jerked the rifle and blasted a shot into the woods. The buck leapt out of sight. Max twisted and jumped to the lip of the gully in one smooth move, slamming the rifle's bolt back and then forward, to load another shell. The strangest-looking cat he'd ever seen jumped straight up, eyeballed him absurdly, then whirled around and scrambled into a grove of laurel bushes.

Max stood with his mouth open in disbelief. Then his old training kicked in, and he noted details. The cat was too big to be domestic, and it had only a stub of a tail. But it didn't look like any bobcat he'd ever seen in these woods. For one thing, it was a brindled color, as if someone had dabbed gray paint on an orange background.

For another, it wore a wide rhinestone collar, and it was missing the paw on its left hind leg.

Details didn't always make sense.

They found Major Templeton in the woods, calling, "Here, kitty, kitty," and muttering about rhinestones.

His jaw set in rigid lines, Max charged after the strange, bumbling, three-footed cat that was trying to run silently through the laurel. He might be going soft, but he wasn't going crazy.

And with his dignity at stake he wasn't going to give up the chase.

Betty Quint crawled from her cave and squinted in the bright afternoon light. She sat back on the heels of her lace-up boots and brushed dirt from her overalls, then adjusted her sock cap. Shielding her eyes with a hand covered in a work glove, she looked up at the sun beaming through golden poplar trees. Good. It couldn't be more than five o'clock. She'd lost track of time and had worried that she'd be walking home in the dusk.

"Relax, city gal, you're safe," she told herself drolly. A gun blast split the silence. In the nanosecond when her heart hid behind her windpipe, Betty heard a *zititip* and then the forceful slap of metal hitting rock. Fragments of granite showered her from a spot high on the cave's face.

Thinking was *such* a bore sometimes, as her mother might have said over Brie and champagne at the country club. Betty put her crawl mechanism into full reverse and scooted backward into the cave. Shaking, she scrambled a dozen feet down the passageway, then crouched in the inky darkness and peered toward the opening.

She heard something running through the woods. It sounded as if it were coming her way fast. Either a hunter had flushed out a deer, or someone was aiming the squirrels and they were attacking.

This was her land, she thought in sudden anger. The first thing she'd done after moving here was post no-hunting signs. This was civilized territory. This was *home*.

Was someone shooting at Faux Paw? Betty gasped and started scrambling toward the cave opening. "Faux, Faux . . ."

But the running feet were Faux Paw's. She bolted into the cave and all twenty pounds of her collided with Betty. "Good cat, good cat," Betty said with relief, trying to stroke her. Faux Paw burst away from her and galloped deeper into the cave. "Faux!" Betty twisted in dismay and listened to Faux Paw's distinctive, three-legged patter fade. The narrow cave entrance opened into a small cavern, and a circuit of man-made tunnels radiated from the back of it.

Betty whipped around to face the opening again when she heard footsteps again—heavier, slower, two legged, deliberate. Her blood froze. Maybe Faux had the right idea. Don't ask questions. Head for the tunnels.

As she began hurriedly backing on hands and knees, a shadow crossed the cave opening. Betty ducked behind a rock outcropping and gazed up the slope in dread. If it was just a hunter, one of the local men, he'd probably apologize profusely for trespassing and scaring her. But she didn't relish the idea of being discovered in the woods alone by an armed man who apparently took potshots at anything that moved.

You don't see the cave opening, she mentally—and firmly—told the shadow. *You want to keep walking. You're leaving. Leave.*

He crouched down in front of the opening. He filled the opening. Betty stared at an unnerving silhouette of large, muscular proportions. He was turned half into the sunlight, and she could make out the green-and-khaki camouflage paint on a brawny forearm he rested on one knee. He wore boots, camouflage pants, and a khaki shirt that hugged his large shoulders and lean middle.

When a glimmer of sunshine caught his face, she saw that it was coated in camouflage paint too. She couldn't define his features or read his expression, but from the fierce way he gripped the huge rifle that was cradled in one arm, she presumed that he was unhappy. "I saw you go in there," he called in a deep, cultured drawl that reverberated through the cave. "And if you think I'm going to let your feisty little tail get away, you're wrong."

Betty clutched the wall. Was he talking to Faux Paw, or to her?

Her breath frozen in her throat, she backed into the cavern and edged across the floor. The man stretched out on his belly and crawled down the passageway, the rifle held in front of him. She watched him merge with the darkness, fade into it, become it. She heard her ragged little attempts to breathe and wondered if he heard them too.

Feeling her way along the cavern wall, she tiptoed to the main tunnel. Her invader made soft scuffling sounds, and she decided that he had risen to his feet. He struck something that made a metallic ring. Betty ducked into the main tunnel and plastered herself against the cold earthen wall. *Don't let him find the lantern,* she prayed.

He found it. The edge of its light flared into the tunnel; Betty nearly tripped over her brogans as she eased down the passage. She stepped through a black rectangle outlined in wood beams. Inside the smaller tunnel she huddled.

She hated this side tunnel. She had decided to take a live-and-let-live attitude with the bats who nested there, but they, ungrateful creatures, now began to squeak loudly at her intrusion. She could hear their wings fluttering as they fretted from their upside-down perches on the ceiling. The floor was slippery with their bad manners.

Betty forgot the bats as measured, slow bootsteps started down the main tunnel toward her. Lantern light danced on the walls. She planted her hands and knees on the nasty floor and crept deeper into the black, cool shaft. She had explored here; she knew that there was nothing to fear in front of her. She had never been fainthearted.

But she'd never been trapped in a cave by Rambo either. She chewed her lower lip and fought to keep her breath from making ragged sounds. Light flared on the wall beside her. He was just outside the entrance to this tunnel. The bats fluttered and squeaked.

Betty forgot decorum and scrambled into the next opening, a larger tunnel, bat free. She glanced over her shoulder and saw light flood the area she'd just left.

The bats left in a rush of wings, and from the muffled curses that accompanied them, at least a few must have taken kamikaze dives at the man blocking their exit.

Betty leapt to her feet and bolted, waving her hands frantically as she tried to find the next opening. She was running out of tunnels, but the next one led back to the cavern, and maybe, just maybe, she could circle back and escape.

Then she heard long, hurried steps behind her. The hair rose on the back of her neck. She tried to think what to do, and realized how unprepared she was.

There hadn't been many courses in hand-to-hand combat at the prestigious women's college she'd attended. And in the eight years since then she'd only had to resort to Kung Fu when someone tried to take her seat at the ballet.

Still, the Quint family was made of hardy pioneer material, and suddenly Betty was sick of scurrying through the darkness like a terrified rat. *The firecrackers. Use the firecrackers.*

She halted, jammed a hand into one voluminous pocket of her overalls, and pulled out a string of delicately misnamed Lady Fingers. She carried them every time she came to work in the cave, just in case something more troublesome than bats had tried to take up residence.

Her teeth chattering with fear, she jerked a lighter from another pocket and lit the fuse.

The bootsteps entered her tunnel. Light streaked toward her. Betty turned around and threw the firecrackers between Rambo's legs.

A small war couldn't have made as much fury and

noise. He jumped and made a heavy thud when his head hit a ceiling beam. He dropped the lantern, and the light curved away from her. She pivoted and ran, bumping into the walls, slipping on the damp stone floor.

To her horror he ran after her. She reached the central cavern and saw the dim light of the exit passage on the other side. *Freedom.*

But Faux Paw decided to head from the tunnels at the same moment. She dashed between Betty's legs and kept going as Betty sprawled sideways. The fall wasn't painful because she landed atop dozens of her carefully nurtured Oriental mushrooms, which grew in a soft bed of dirt and dried horse manure.

The discomfort came a moment later, when a thick masculine knee settled on her fanny and a strong hand grabbed the back of her neck. With her cheek pressed into the odiferous humus and flattened mushrooms, she gasped for breath and exploded with fury.

"Off me! Off me! Dammit."

"Kid, you play dangerous games," he said. "When I tell your daddy what you're up to, he'll probably chew your ass."

"My cave. My land."

"Cut the crap. What have you got stashed in here?"

"Have you . . . arrested. Off me!"

He didn't hurt her, but his fingers curled tighter around her neck. "I came in here after an animal. I didn't expect to find—what? What are you growing in here, kid? Don't lie. It won't do you any good."

Betty ignored her terror enough to consider her options. She suspected that he wouldn't listen to pleas of innocence. He thought she was a juvenile delinquent, and whether he thought she was male or female wasn't clear. She wasn't going to enlighten him. At least he was taking a paternal attitude. She was a little reassured, but not much.

Her stubborn silence seemed the best offense. She ground her teeth and refused to talk to him.

After a minute he sighed in exasperation. "All right, here's the way we're going to do this. You won't like it, but it will make my life easier." She heard unidentifiable sounds, then discerned the slap of a belt being removed from its belt loops. A second later he deftly grabbed her right hand with his free hand and looped the belt around it.

"No!" she yelled. "No way!"

Flapping arms when pinned facedown didn't offer much defense. But still he quickly scooped her hands together and bound them behind her back. "Okay, kid, let's take a trip to the sunshine."

He stood, wrapped his hand in the back of her overalls, and dragged her gracefully out of the mushroom bed and onto the granite floor.

She was so mad now that she didn't care what happened. As he pulled her along beside him like a large piece of luggage, Betty craned her head sideways and tried to bite his knee.

He shook her a little and moved out of range. "I'll remember that, kid," he assured her.

When they reached the narrow passageway to the opening, he halted. "On your belly," he ordered, as if she had a choice. But he lowered her gently. "Crawl. I'll be right behind you."

Humiliated, her fanny poking into the air every time she drew a leg forward to push herself, she wiggled up the smooth stone slope. Her tormentor crawled so close behind her that his hands brushed her hips and legs.

Betty pushed herself out of the cave onto the matted grass and leaves of the forest floor. Frightened, angry, sputtering for breath, she twisted on her side and glared at him. He seemed huge. The rifle hung by a webbed strap from one of his thick shoulders. A sick realization of just how small and helpless she was in comparison made her burst into self-defense.

With a hoarse cry of rage she raised a booted foot and kicked him in the shoulder. He made no sound but moved with lethal speed. Rearing on his knees, he

grabbed her feet with his hands and flipped her onto her back. Then he put one hand on her stomach and one on her throat.

Slowly he bent over her until his camouflage-painted nose was only inches from her dirt-smeared one. The look in his eyes, startling in their intensity and surrounded by the dark camouflage colors, was vivid with controlled fury. "I could rip your tonsils out with my fingernails," he whispered between gritted teeth. And then his threats became *really* colorful.

Betty stared up at him as he continued to whisper about chewing and gouging and kicking various parts of her anatomy. There was no doubt from some of his references that he thought she was male. But no man had ever talked to her in this violent, lurid way before, and her dignity rebelled.

"What do you think I am?" she yelled back at him. She dug the back of her head into the ground and scrubbed her cap off. "I'm a woman, you idiot! You're mauling and cursing a woman! Is this your idea of gallantry? You trespass on my land, shoot at me, trap me in my own cave, and then yell at me? You big macho bastard!"

He froze. Then he sat back on his heels and regarded her with a fathomless expression. His gaze moved over the bulky gray sweatshirt and denim overalls. He reached out and flicked the clasp open on one strap of the overalls' bib, then pulled the bib aside and scrutinized her chest.

"Oh, don't," she said in horror.

He jerked his hand back. "That's not what I meant." He flung the bib into place and groaned in disgust. "I just wanted to make sure that you were a woman. But you're not just a woman, you're a stealth bomber with a bosom."

"Funny."

He reached over a second time and wiped grime from her face. "I must be getting old. Hell, yes, you're very female." He looked closely at her shoulder-length black

hair. Then, muttering an oath of self-rebuke under his breath, he turned her onto her stomach and quickly freed her hands.

Relief shuddered through her. She whipped around, shoved herself upright with one hand, and slapped him across the face with the other. He barely blinked. "Okay. I deserved that."

Betty scooted several feet away from him. "What gives you the right to manhandle someone who's minding her own business?" she demanded raggedly.

His eyes were light green. They never wavered from hers. "There was no reason for anyone to be in that cave. I thought you were a kid hiding drugs. Why didn't you come out when I called you?"

"I can't imagine where my manners were. I *always* respond when I'm given orders by strange men in military gear carrying big rifles. Why did you shoot at me?"

"I didn't shoot at you. I was aiming at a deer."

"A ten-foot-tall deer."

"Some kind of strange bobcat ran into me, and my shot went bad. I swear. I tracked the cat here."

"It's my pet!"

He did a double take, then recovered. "Calm down. I wasn't planning to make a rug out of it. I only wanted to get a better look at the thing." Lifting a dirty hand, he pointed at her to emphasize his next intense words. "I would never hunt where it wasn't safe to shoot. I thought this land was empty."

"It's not empty. It's mine. And there are no-hunting signs posted everywhere."

"I walked in from the south. You didn't post them there."

"But . . . but there's no road on that side for at least ten miles. That's why I never thought anyone would wander over my boundaries from that direction."

He shrugged. The rifle rode the heavy muscles of his back. "I like to hike," he said simply. He cleared his throat. "You can file assault charges against me. I do owe you an apology, and it's sincere. Will you accept?"

His honesty caught her off guard. The way his gaze kept flickering over her face and body distracted her. Betty wiped a gloved hand to her face and wondered if she looked awful. "I'm supposed to just grin and say, 'Aw, shucks, Rambo, no harm done'?"

"You have to admit, there were extenuating circumstances." Admiration grew in his eyes as he studied her. "You were damned good in that cave. Resourceful."

Betty realized that she was adorning her cheek with bat guano. She dropped her hand into her lap. *He has beautiful green eyes,* she couldn't help thinking. And his hair, now that she could finally see it, was a rich almond shade of brown. And all the camouflage in the world couldn't disguise a finely honed masculine body in its prime.

"Who are you?" she asked.

"Where do you live?" he countered.

"Who are you?" she repeated.

"You never accepted my apology."

"I don't accept apologies from nameless strangers."

"Max Templeton. I'd offer to shake hands, but I doubt you're in the mood."

"You're right. Are you local?"

"Lately, yes."

"Good. Then you'll feel at home in the local jail."

"You're not making this apology process easy."

"You trespassed on my property and assaulted me."

"Don't forget a misdemeanor charge concerning the careless use of a firearm."

"You're not taking this seriously."

"You tossed a handful of firecrackers between my legs. I'm too upset to think straight."

"You don't look upset."

"You don't look upset either. Let's go have a beer and get acquainted. I'll buy. My apology will be much more acceptable with a froth on it."

She slumped. A ticklish new fear sat in the bottom of her chest, the fear that something potent was brewing between the two of them. Flights of fancy and reckless

behavior were a bad combination, she knew from past experience.

"Just take another hike," she told him. "Back where you came from. And don't trespass on my land again."

"What were you doing inside that cave?"

"Growing mushrooms." She gave him a rebuking look. "Ordinary, edible mushrooms."

"You have pieces of mushroom on your sweatshirt."

She glanced down at her gray shirt and winced. A lot of work had been mashed. "Great."

"I'll pay you for damages."

"Forget it. Just leave."

"This cave is called Quint's Hideout. Back in the early nineteen-hundreds a local named William Quint mined gold in it. Later he made moonshine here."

"I know. I'm his granddaughter. I own the cave now."

"You mean—" he glanced toward the north. "You bought the Quint place?"

"That's right."

"There hasn't been a Quint around here for fifty years. The house belonged to the Gibson family, the last I heard. And none of them live here anymore either."

"Right. It's been vacant for a few years. I just bought the place from the Gibsons."

"It must be in terrible shape."

"No worse than my nerves at the moment."

"You look steady. I'm impressed. And apologetic. Really. I'll walk you home, and you can explain why you love mushrooms so much." He leaned toward her with disarming effect and smiled. "I live just north of town. We're practically neighbors."

"I can walk myself. It's just over the ridge. And if I ever see you on my land again, I'll call the sheriff."

"Your lantern is still burning inside the cave. Wait here." He took the gun from his back, laid it on the ground at her feet like a warrior surrendering his sword, then slid into the cave opening. "Be right back."

Betty numbly tugged her gloves off, then used her cap to wipe her face. So he thought she looked steady?

Her hands were trembling, and inside she was nothing but a tangle of questions. Max Templeton. Max. She mouthed the name. He was local. She'd see him again. The thought gave her a trill of excitement along with dismay.

A throaty, plaintive *meow* caught her attention. Betty looked toward the tall stump of a dead tree. Faux sat there, a wary expression on her face. "Come here, baby. It's all right." The brindle cat leapt down and trotted to her, using the stump of its hind leg almost as gracefully as a foot.

Faux crawled into her lap and curled up, her body spilling out over Betty's knees. Her tufted ears twitched at the sounds of Max Templeton's return. "It's all right, Faux," Betty assured her, stroking her head. "I *hope* so, anyway."

Max Templeton shoved himself half out of the cave, then spotted Faux and halted, his eyes narrowing in scrutiny. "The stealth cat," he said gruffly. "What kind of cat is it?"

"Half bobcat, half Manx. The product of a very strange romance."

Betty's attention was riveted to him. He must be over six feet tall, almost a head taller than she. The paint had begun to streak on his face, accenting the hard thrust of his chin but also curving around the sensual lines of his mouth. His nose was straight and chiseled; his eyes were large. It was a surprisingly elegant face in contrast to a brutally handsome body. A unique and troublesome combination.

Betty set Faux Paw down and rose to her feet. Max Templeton stood also, and she discovered that she had been right—he was a good six inches taller than she. "Ms. Quint," he said politely. "Your cave is secure. Your strange cat is safe. You're not hurt. Will you accept my apology?"

He could sound so formal. He had a very straight-backed, chin-up posture. His voice had the light drawl of a southerner who'd spent a lot of years away from

home. It wasn't as crisp as her voice, with its urban-Atlanta lilt, but it wasn't gruff and twangy, the way the natives talked up here.

"Please accept my apology," he repeated, gazing at her curiously. "Are you all right?"

Distracted, she nodded. "This was obviously just one of life's fiascos. A quirk of coincidence and misunderstanding. I accept your apology."

"Does this mean that I'm allowed to learn your first name?"

"Betty."

"Nice. I've never known a Betty before."

"Not one under eighty years old, at least. It's not a fashionable name anymore."

"Were you named after a relative?"

"No. My father insists that I was named after Betty Rubble, on *The Flintstones*."

"I think I'd like your father. And what's the stealth cat's name?"

"Faux Paw. It's a play on the French phrase *faux pas*, which means—"

"I know." He looked at her with mild rebuke. "Yes'm, I done learned a little French myself."

"Sorry. I was just—"

"Judging a book by its camouflage."

She shifted awkwardly, feeling like a nervous teen-ager under his assertive attention. "I'm sorry. Good-bye. Meeting you was an interesting experience."

"I take it that now is not the time to say that you look great in dirty overalls and that you're very pretty despite the bat poop on your face. Or that I'd like to take you to dinner tonight."

"That's right."

"Bad timing. I'll try again later." He picked up his rifle and hitched the strap over his shoulder. "Well, it's a long hike back to my Jeep. If you change your mind about filing charges, you can find me in Webster Springs."

"I accepted your apology. I don't go back on my acceptances." She couldn't resist. "Do you work in town?"

"At the courthouse. Part-time. Monday through Friday, nine to one." He nodded to her graciously, but his eyes were less subtle as he scanned her one last time from head to toe. "And where can I find you?"

"At the old Colton house. Right off the square."

"You bought one house in town and another outside of town?"

"I'm turning the Colton place into a restaurant. I'm a professional caterer. I'm expanding my business."

"Terrific. I'll see you again. Soon."

Very soon, she suspected, and her mouth went dry.

He nodded to her. "Good-bye, Betty. Au revoir, Faux Paw." Smiling, he started into the woods.

"What kind of work do *you* do?" Betty called.

He turned, framed by the beautiful golden poplar trees, imprinting himself on her mind forever. His smile widened, cheerful and irresistible despite his harshly painted face. "I'm the justice of the peace."

He pivoted and walked away whistling, while Betty stared after him in astonishment.

Two

"He really is the justice of the peace," Grace Larson told her as they watched workmen fit a stainless steel smoker into a niche of the restaurant's kitchen wall. Grace, trim and neat in designer jeans, a gold-braided belt, and a cashmere sweater, was the mayor's wife. She was also head of the chamber of commerce and the owner of the clothing shop next door to Betty's restaurant.

"The state legislature changed things a few years ago," Grace continued. "The position is really called 'magistrate' now, but it's the same as justice of the peace. Max was elected last month. His father was justice of the peace in this county for more than forty years." Grace stroked a gray curl coyly and laughed. "Bartram Templeton was a legend, let me tell you."

Betty, her jeans and workshirt already coated with a film of dust, frowned as she knocked more dust into the air while scrubbing a countertop. "A good legend or a bad legend?"

"Depends on your point of view. If you were the husband of one of Bartram's lady friends, you might say it was a bad legend."

Betty halted and stared at her. "Are we talking 'town lecher' here?"

"No, honey, we're talking 'town Romeo' here. Bartram never stole a heart that didn't want to be stolen."

"He cheated on his wife, Max's mother?"

"Oh, no. She died when Max was a baby. Some people say she was the only woman Bartram ever loved—he didn't get married until he was over forty, and after she died, he never married again. Didn't stop him from having a good time, though." Grace smiled. "Before I was married, I had a few dates with him myself. He was very hard to forget."

"Then why—"

"He wasn't the marrying kind. I was."

"So Max grew up here with an aging playboy for a father."

"Uh huh. Max cut a pretty wide path through the local girls himself, though he was no match for his daddy. After he graduated from high school, he joined the marines, and I bet we didn't see him more than a handful of times after that. Just when he'd visit Bartram. Last winter he came back for his daddy's funeral and then, a few months later, he came back for good."

Grace bent her head closer so the workmen couldn't hear. "Bartram was over eighty years old. But he died in the saddle, if you know what I mean."

Betty swallowed a smile. "Any horse I'd know?"

Grace nodded. "Connie Jean Brown."

"Not the grandmotherly little lady who runs the yogurt shop!"

"The same. Thank goodness her husband didn't get upset. I think he was sort of proud of Connie Jean for being a sexy senior citizen."

Betty slumped against the counter and tossed her brush down. She couldn't help laughing. "Grace, I moved up here to get back to basics, to live in a place where most people still believe in traditional values. If Bartram Templeton's escapades are the kinkiest gossip you've got, then I'm happy. That's a great story."

Grace laughed too. "This'll make it even better then. Do you know what Bartram did besides working as justice of the peace? Ever hear of the Hitching Post?"

"Hmmm. I vaguely remember an article in one of the

Atlanta magazines about a strange little business up here—"

"That was it. Bartram ran it." Grace grinned. "And Max just reopened it."

Betty crossed her arms over her chest and eyed Grace grimly. "You mean that he runs a wedding chapel? He marries people?"

Grace hooted. "Yes, honey. You make it sound like he marries them to himself." She raised a gray eyebrow rakishly. "We call it a wedding *parlor*, not a chapel. If Max Templeton is like his daddy, his weddings are like no weddings you've ever seen before. Do you know how people get married at that parlor?"

Betty stared at her wide-eyed. "How?"

"They get married in costumes. I mean, if they want to. There's an extra fee for it. Civil War, Indian, pioneer— even got a suit of armor one of the local welders made. The groom can dress up like a knight. If Max runs the place the same as his daddy did, getting married is a big joke."

"That's awful."

"I sort of think so too." Grace looked at her curiously. "But you look really upset."

"I think weddings should be dignified. I think marriage is too important to be treated as a joke." Betty hesitated, then admitted softly, "I'm a recent dropout of the 'we-don't-need-a-formal-commitment' school of relationships. Trust me, it's a tough course. I believe in marriage. I think that it's still the most loving and most dedicated way to live."

Grace patted her hand in consolation. "Honey, you're gonna find yourself a good ol' boy up here who'll marry you in a second. You're only thirty years old. You got a few good years left."

"Well, thanks."

"Just don't get involved with Max Templeton unless you want a good time but not much else."

"I've had that kind of good time already. It wasn't so good." Betty had barely finished grinding her teeth before the delivery boy arrived.

"Present for Ms. Quint," he announced, standing in the doorway of the restaurant's screened veranda.

Betty stared at the basket he carried. It was wrapped in a florist's colorful cellophane and topped by a large red bow. It was filled with mushrooms. "Who's this from?" she asked, although the answer loomed in her mind.

"Here's the card, ma'am."

After the boy left, she set the basket on a table and read the car's message. *Don't keep me in the dark*, the thick, bold script cajoled. *I owe you a dinner.* It was signed by Max, of course, and included his telephone number.

Grace peered over her shoulder. "Oh, Lord," she whispered in awe. "Max Templeton is after you. The legend lives on."

The young couple looked good dressed up as Scarlett and Rhett, Max thought. He'd given them a discount on the costume fee because they were just twenty-one, and from the looks of the boy's ancient sports car, they didn't have much money.

But business was business. He didn't want to work more than three nights a week and an occasional Saturday, so he had to keep a tight schedule. He'd just reopened the parlor two weeks ago, and he hadn't done any advertising besides a notice in the Webster Springs paper, but word had gotten around fast.

Scarlett and Rhett were his six o'clock couple; at six forty-five he had a thirtyish pair who had already married and divorced each other two times, each marriage courtesy of his father, and now they were going for number three. They wanted the medieval outfit—a dress straight out of *Camelot* for her, armor for him. In this case, maybe both of them should wear armor.

At seven-thirty he had a couple who wanted nothing but the plain package—no costumes, one round of the wedding march on the parlor organ, and a gilt-edged

certificate. At eighty-thirty he had another plain package, except that the couple wanted the ceremony videotaped, so he had to take time to set up the equipment.

After that he'd give Norma a hug good night, walk to his weathered old house on the hill above the parlor, and check the answering machine for a message from the fascinating Betty Quint. The thought made him impatient.

He stepped from his carpeted platform for a second and leaned across the organ. Norma Bishop peered at him over her bifocals, her expression stern. Max bent his head beside Norma's grizzled Afro and whispered in her ear, "Step on the gas."

"I was playing the wedding march on this organ when you were still sucking your thumb. Get your butt back where it belongs. And straighten your tie."

Grinning, Max went back to the platform. He slid a hand over the black string tie he wore with his marrying outfit—a Templeton tradition, black boots, black trousers, a long-tailed black coat, a stiff white shirt, and a string tie. It was the country-judge look, his father had always said. People liked it.

Scarlett and Rhett were halfway down the aisle between rows of folding wooden chairs, only a few of which were occupied by their friends. Scarlett's hoop skirt got caught on a chair, and as she tugged it loose Max made a mental note to widen the aisle a bit.

The double doors at the back of the parlor opened just enough for Betty Quint to squeeze through. She slipped quietly into the last row of chairs and studied the scene with wide eyes. Gray eyes, Max recalled instantly, straightening and staring at her in pleased surprise. Eyes the color of pewter.

Since their encounter two days ago she'd traded her mushroom clothes for soft-gray slacks and a Nordic-looking sweater of grays and blues. Without the overalls it was even more clear that she was slender, athletic looking, and the owner of some terrific curves.

He hair was a burnished black with auburn high-

lights, and it was gently layered from bangs in the front to gleaming curves that clung to the tops of her shoulders. She had an offbeat face, angular and serious, but it was softened by wide, full lips and those big gray eyes hooded in black lashes.

Those eyes met his with rueful humor and more than a little disgust. She gave him a once-over that made the hair stand up all over his body, a significant effect, considering the amount of hair he had. Of course he knew she was trying to wither him, not flatter him.

He nodded to her; she responded with a frosty smile. As Scarlett and Rhett plodded up the aisle Max did a brief mental inventory of the information he'd garnered on Betty Quint today. The merchants in town claimed that she was outgoing, businesslike, and very nice.

She'd moved here a month ago, buying the old family home and fifty acres of meadow and woodland along with it. She'd grown up in Atlanta—her father, John Quint, had left Webster Springs as a young man and made a fortune in the Atlanta real estate market.

She was an award-winning barbecue caterer, and she was going to continue that business as well as run her restaurant in town. She was eight years younger than he, definitely single, and she lived alone—except for the stealth cat—in her ramshackle new home.

Max drew his attention away from her as Scarlett and Rhett reached the end of the aisle and stopped, their hands clasped together tightly, their young faces shining with a mixture of anticipation and awkwardness. Norma hit the last notes of the wedding march, then sat with her dark hands folded patiently on the lap of her blue woolen dress, a solemn expression on her face.

Max married the couple with style, embellishing the official wording of the legal language with some quotes from Oriental philosophy he'd picked up during an assignment in Japan. He suppressed a yawn as he talked about blooming together in perfect harmony. He was proud of his wit. By merely changing the lotus-

blossom references to dogwood blossoms, he gave the quotes a southern flavor.

The couple exchanged rings, smiled tearfully at each other, and kissed for about five minutes after he pronounced them husband and wife. Max glanced over their heads at Betty Quint and found a pensive, unguarded expression on her face. She was watching Scarlett and Rhett, her head tilted to one side, her mouth set in a sad bow.

Her sentimental attitude puzzled Max. He wondered if she'd been married once and was musing over unhappy memories. Or that maybe she found it sad to watch two fresh-faced youngsters throw themselves into a partnership that would probably fall apart when they matured.

But when the pair tromped back down the aisle to the accompaniment of Norma's organ music, Betty Quint bounded up and opened the parlor doors for them, then stood aside and smiled at them as they went into the anteroom.

Max stared a moment, then regained his concentration. "There will be a brief reception," he told the couple's friends. "Please follow the bride and groom to the After— To the reception room to the right."

As the guests hurried out Max continued to watch Betty Quint. His concentration was still muddled—he'd almost called the reception room by his private name for it. The Aftershock Bunker.

"Nice job," Norma allowed to Max. She turned her stout frame on the organ bench and smiled mischievously at Betty Quint. "Come on in, Betty. You interested in making an appointment?"

Max watched with fascination as Betty blinked tears away, straightened, and became neutral again. She smiled at Norma. "I'm just an innocent spectator. I had to see this for myself. I hope you don't mind." Her gaze switched to Max. "I considered the mushroom basket a kind of invitation."

"Glad to have you." He nodded and stepped down off

the platform as she walked up the aisle. There was something compelling about the structured man-meeting-woman design of the aisle; he felt as if she were being directed to him, and he found himself unable to look away from her somber gray eyes.

"What did you think?" he asked bluntly. She came to a stop and stood looking up at him with intense scrutiny, as if trying to read his mind.

"I think you don't take your position very seriously. You're encouraging people to make fun of a very profound moment in their lives." She glanced at Norma. "I'm sorry, Mrs. Bishop. Don't hold this against me when my business license comes up for renewal before the city council."

Norma, who had served on the town council for two decades, dismissed the worry with a gracious wave of one hand. "This kind of wedding isn't for everyone. But married is married. Those that are gonna make it will make it no matter what kind of ceremony they have."

"That's right," Max added, feeling a little annoyed. The Hitching Post was a longtime local tradition. The chamber of commerce had *asked* him to reopen it. It drew tourists, who came to snap pictures in front of the tiny old Victorian house with its sweeping water oaks and the aging sign that flashed "Get Hitched" in red neon over the front-porch steps.

"You might be interested to know that I don't own this place. Norma does," he told Betty Quint. "My father willed it to her."

"If you want to see some *real* strange things, stay around tonight and watch a medieval wedding," Norma added. "Sometimes the groom trips over his armor."

Max stepped a little closer to Betty, pushing a little, testing the waters. He'd never wanted to test the waters so badly in his life, he realized. "Why don't you stay and watch? I'm doing three more ceremonies tonight, but I'll be finished by nine. Then we could go over to the steak house and have a late dinner."

Betty Quint's complexion was Irish cream, and exasperation showed in it easily. "No, thank you. I just wanted you to know that the mushroom basket was a nice gesture, your apology is *definitely* accepted, and the incident is closed."

Max took another step. "Then why not have dinner with me?"

Norma rose from her bench and said diplomatically, "I better go see about keeping Scarlett and Rhett on schedule. You hustle on over to the reception before long, Maximilian, and let's sign their certificate."

"Yes, ma'am. I'll be there in a second."

"Nice to see you again, Mrs. Bishop," Betty said politely. "I want to come by when you have more time. I hear you have some pretty queen-size quilts for sale."

"Always do. And you're always welcome. I'm always here. Upstairs." Norma left the parlor with a spry, forceful gate, her heavy arms pumping.

"Nice lady," Betty noted. She took a step back from Max. "She seems to have a way with you. Remarkable."

"She's the heart of this place. She keeps the appointment books, takes care of the costumes, orders me around like a sergeant at boot camp. I grew up being best friends with her son, and we joined the marines together. He was killed in Vietnam. She and I sort of adopted each other after that." Max leaned toward her. "But enough chitchat. You smell wonderful. Tangy."

"I've been making barbecue sauce."

"Mmmm. I'm a rib man." He let his gaze travel down her chest, then back up.

"Mine are hickory smoked."

"Must have been painful."

She was breathing a little too fast now, and he liked the way her nostrils flared a bit each time she inhaled. She frowned at him. "My restaurant will open soon. Chicken, pork, and beef barbecue. Chopped or sliced. Sandwiches or plates. Eat-in or carry-out. Stop by on the first day. I'll be giving away free samples."

"I like free samples."

"I bet."

He grasped his chest woefully. "You don't approve of me."

"Not since you invaded my cave and mashed my face into mushrooms and manure."

"I admit, it's not the usual way I'd want to meet a woman. But I don't think you're my usual kind of woman."

"Oh? You mean because I don't wear leather underwear or have skulls tattooed on my forearms?"

He laughed, liking the way her eyes never left him despite her anger. "First of all, because you're a civilian. Second, because you're refusing to have dinner with me—women *never* do that. Third, because yesterday you were a helluva lot more angry than frightened. I've known some pretty warlike women, but they were trained to be that way. With you, it just comes naturally. Very appealing."

"I'd like to ask you a personal question."

"Hmmm. Go ahead."

"Why are you running loose in the real world? I understand that you retired from the marines with the rank of major. Sounds like an unwise time to leave a career, to me."

Her face was pink with annoyance. He wanted to touch it and feel the heat of her emotions under his fingertips. He wanted to take her to dinner, then take her to bed. Funny, she was a newcomer here, but suddenly he realized that she was the homecoming he needed.

"I wanted to see if I could do something new with my life. See if I remembered how to be a civilian. Apparently, you had the same need to do something new. Why leave the bright lights of Atlanta and move to a little tourist town in the mountains?"

"I wanted to find something more innocent, and kind, and traditional about life."

"A honey of a plan. I approve. But my whole career was built on tradition, and I think a person has to be

careful not to let tradition give him a rigid, narrow perspective on life."

"I think you're talking about tradition as in *rules*. I'm talking about *values*."

"Right at the moment I don't care what we're talking about. I'm just glad you came by to see me." He gave in to the compelling desire to touch her, carefully resting one hand on one of her arms, letting his fingertips press just tight enough to feel her arm beneath the sweater. The contact burned him, made him want to draw her forward and whisper before he kissed her, *Let's start some new traditions.*

She looked down at her captured arm, but didn't pull away. Her eyes revealed alarm, though she gave him a jaunty, patronizing smile. "You plan to add me to your harem?"

After a moment of surprise he smiled wickedly. "The reports of my harem are greatly exaggerated. In fact, I think if you'll check around—which you've obviously begun doing already—you'll learn that in the last six months I've been rather tame."

"Breaking your father's tradition, Mr. Templeton?"

He pulled her into his arms quickly and looked down into her startled eyes. "My father had his faults, but he was a good man."

She locked her hands on his shoulders and tried to push herself away. "He must have been *very* good. He made a *lot* of women happy. Some of them were married to other men at the time."

"Chasing married women isn't my style. There are plenty of the unattached kind. But, I admit, I did inherit my father's ability to make women happy. Only I've been a little reluctant to take up the torch of the family legend. Pa left quite a reputation."

"I wouldn't want to waste your time."

"You'd never be a waste. How about that free sample?"

He kissed her before she could answer, his mouth skilled against her resistance, coaxing, careful. What he'd meant to be a provocative tease became a searing

discovery. The taste, the feel, and the scent of her shattered his playfulness.

She made a fierce sound in the back of her throat; she clutched his black coat with knotted hands and braced her arms against him. But at the same time her body began to sag toward his, her breasts flattening against his chest, her back arching. He heard her soft cry of dismay as her mouth softened under his and became mobile. When he flicked his tongue forward, she caught it between the edges of her lips, then groaned with defeat and opened her mouth for his quick thrust.

Dazed and reckless, Max bent her backward. To his delight her arms went around his neck. She was grabbing at him instinctively, as her balance now depended on him, but when her hands splayed across his shoulders with an exploring touch, he knew she'd lost her footing in more ways than one.

He slid his arms around her shoulders and waist while he continued to twist his mouth on hers. She shivered against him and returned his intimate exploration, her tongue quick and desperate, like the mood that had overwhelmed them.

The hearty applause from the parlor doorway broke the spell. Max drew his head up, frowning, and saw Scarlett, Rhett, all their friends, and Norma. Norma rolled her eyes as if she'd caught a pair of children playing a naughty game.

Betty Quint, who lay helpless inside his arms with her knees buckled and her body draped over one of his legs, regained her control with a breathless groan of disbelief. Jerking her arms from around his neck, she shoved him hard and twisted violently at the same time.

Max was just starting to lift her. The end result was that she slipped from his arms and plopped on her rump, half-sitting on the toes of his black boots. Her sweater bunched under her arms during the trip down. Max studied her bare midriff and bent over to help her straighten the sweater. She scooted away from him, her eyes flashing, her face as red as a sourwood leaf.

There were cheers from the audience. Max frowned harder and motioned to Norma to close the doors as he extended a hand to Betty. But Betty scrambled to her feet, jerked her sweater into place, and said low enough that only he could hear, "Set one foot in my restaurant and I'll come after you with a carving knife."

"You're overreacting."

"You aren't in the marines anymore. I'm not some military objective you have to take at all costs. I'm not interested in a man who thinks he can have what he wants no matter what the consequences. Go play cute with someone else."

"I wasn't playing cute. Smooth your feathers and have a seat. Let's talk. Something is happening between us, and it's shaking me up too—"

"The Braselton's are here early," Norma called from the door. "You have to help me get the suit of armor out."

Betty laughed wearily and shook her head. "Stay here and talk to you? I'd have to be desperate or crazy. And I'm not either one."

Max rocked on his heels and eyed her with challenge. "From the way you kissed me, you were desperate for something."

"Not for you." She pivoted gracefully and strode from the parlor. Scarlett and Rhett stopped holding hands just long enough for her to pass between them.

She might have to suffer for a while, but eventually the old Quint place was going to be a terrific home. She was certain. If she could only keep the possum from creeping into her bedroom at night.

Betty peeked over the electric blanket. In the dim glow of a night-light the possum scuttled along one wall. It was a funny-ugly animal, and it hurried as if embarrassed to be in her boudoir. From a spot at the foot of the bed, Faux Paw craned her head slightly, fur rising as she watched the intruder.

Having been defanged, declawed, and neutered by her previous owner—the same one who had dumped her on the doorstep of the Atlanta Humane Society with an injured hind foot—Faux Paw was a rather nonchalant predator. After the possum disappeared into the hallway she yawned.

Betty settled back on big pillows encased in white silk and listened to the brisk October wind whisper around the eaves. The house creaked, and it smelled of old wood and the pungent pine fire she'd built in the downstairs fireplace after supper. An electric heater hummed in one corner of her bedroom. The smells and sounds were all cozy, and when she shut her eyes, she could picture the place when the remodeling was done.

There wouldn't be sawhorses and paint cans in the upstairs hallway or muddy two-by-sixes covering a hole in the front porch. The big living room downstairs would be filled with Early American antiques, and the big kitchen would be a gourmet's playground instead of an empty shell lined with cracked linoleum and peeling wallpaper. The possum wouldn't have his secret passageways into her bedroom.

Trading her pleasant condominium in Atlanta for this place had been an impulsive decision. Her father had criticized her for putting whimsy ahead of logic, and her mother had given her a "That's nice, dear" in between social events. Typical. She never counted on them for support.

Betty tugged the blanket up to her nose and frowned in drowsy thought. She had learned to take care of herself at an early age. She'd survived some tough times. Max Templeton was in for a shock if he thought she was a pushover.

She tried to force him out of her mind even as the memory of his hot, skilled mouth made her stomach drop. She didn't want to dream about his kiss, or the way his arms had felt around her, or the dark, dashing figure he had cut in his black outfit.

She'd always pictured marines as being stern, strait-

laced, and humorless. How could cheerfully lecherous Max Templeton be the man who, according to Grace, had gone to Vietnam as a sergeant but come back a first lieutenant, having won a battlefield commission for saving his platoon during an ambush?

Recalling his cool, lethal power as he'd dragged her from the cave, she knew there was more to him than she'd imagined. Betty frowned sleepily. She'd imagined a great deal. There was too much to him, too much that was tempting.

She'd just begun to doze when her ears caught the sound of a vehicle coming up the narrow gravel road. Betty climbed from bed and ran to the window. A silver half-moon showed the rock-spewing arrival of a Jeep traveling too fast. It roared down her drive between an old meadow on one side and forest on the other, then slid to a stop a few feet from the overgrown nandinas at the edge of the front walk.

Betty watched in consternation as a tall dim figure vaulted from the Jeep and strode toward her front porch. By the time she threw a heavy robe over her pajamas and ran down the staircase, the visitor was knocking loudly on the front odor.

She switched the porch light on and pulled back the white blanket that covered a window near the door. Max Templeton. Of course.

Three

He was dressed in hiking boots, loose tan trousers, and a woolen poncho of bright yellow, white, and red.

Betty opened the door wearily and frowned up at him. "Don't tell me. You're testing a Mexican-bandit theme for the wedding parlor. Nice serape you've got there."

He ran a hand over his ruffled brown hair and gave her a grim look in return. His face had its share of mature lines and creases, emphasized now by his tense expression. There was nothing playful about him. "The sheriff is looking for three men who just robbed Ralph's."

"Ralph's? The all-night convenience store up at the intersection?"

"Yes. A deputy was on patrol nearby and he chased their car this way. It ran off the road a few yards to the south of your driveway, and the three of them headed into the woods."

Betty pulled the soft-blue lapels of her robe closer over her throat. "And they haven't been caught yet?"

"No."

"How did you—"

"I was playing cards with the night dispatcher at the sheriff's office when the call came in." He glanced down the porch at the tall living room windows that until

recently had been boarded over. "You need new windows with better locks. These things are flimsy."

"I know that. I'm having them replaced."

"I'll be right back." He walked to the Jeep, pulled something large and bulky out of the front passenger seat, and carried it back to the porch. It was a sleeping bag. "Got a couch?"

"Wait a minute—"

"Don't tell me to go home. I'll just sleep on the porch and make you feel guilty. Let me come in. It's windy out here."

"How do I know that you aren't making this little drama up?"

A wicked, melodramatic laugh rolled from his throat. "I have more subtle ways of luring unsuspecting women into my clutches. If you want to confirm my story, call the sheriff's office."

"All right. I will." She continued to block the doorway, her defenses on alert against the teasing smile. But his eyes looked tired, and his attitude was ruffled, like his hair. He seemed harried, not devious. "Come in."

"Oh, thank you, thank you."

While he locked the front door, she went to a phone perched on a stack of cookbooks on a heavy rosewood table, practically the only furnishing in the downstairs rooms. She switched on a lamp and called the sheriff's office, where someone named Ray Jay told her that, yes, three armed men had robbed the convenience store and were being hunted near her property.

"Is Max Templeton there yet?" Ray Jay asked.

"Uhmmm, yes."

"I'll call if we get more information."

"Thank you."

Feeling guilty, Betty put the phone down and turned slowly to look at Max. He lounged against the arching frame of the living room entrance, watching her, his expression neither smug nor rebuking. Betty nodded to him. "I apologize."

"Accepted."

"As you can see, I have practically no furniture."

He rubbed the toe of his hiking boot along the scarred oak floor. "Nice finish. Looks like the cavalry rode through."

"At least twice."

"A hard, cold floor. I'm glad I have an air mattress."

"Max, you don't owe me—"

"And I didn't ask for anything in return, now did I?"

They traded a somber, searching gaze. Her instincts told her to ignore the jolt of desire that ran through her. He could be gallant all he wanted, but he simply wasn't the kind of man she'd let herself covet. Still, the look in his eyes was making her knees weak. "How about a cup of hot chocolate with a shot of bourbon in it?" she asked.

"Are you going to have one?"

"Yes. The hot chocolate, not the bourbon." *I have to keep a clear head.*

"Then I'll take a virgin hot chocolate too."

"I've never heard it put quite that way before."

"I've always had a colorful vocabulary."

"I know. You used it on me in the woods the other day."

"In the marines you learn a lot of interesting ways to communicate with people."

"What did you do—teach grunt-speak to the troops?"

He bowed slightly. "I was an intelligence officer. I commanded an antiterrorist team. I hope you're suitably impressed."

"Frankly, I am."

"Does this softening of your heart mean that I can visit your restaurant without fear?"

"Don't push your luck." She gestured toward his sleeping bag. "Use some of that hot air and blow up your mattress. I'll get the hot chocolate."

"I've owned sabers that weren't as sharp as your tongue."

She curtsied. "Thank you."

In the kitchen, distracted and tense, she nearly dropped the two mugs she removed from the cardboard box that contained a spartan set of stoneware dishes. Standing at the sink under a bare light bulb that hung from the ceiling on a cord, she filled the mugs and put them in the microwave oven. A sink, a microwave oven, and a small rented refrigerator—that was her kitchen.

"The uncluttered look," Max said from the doorway.

She jumped. "You walk softly."

"And carry a big stick." He had removed the poncho, and she saw that he wore a loose black pullover with his trousers. Again she was captivated by his big-shouldered, long-legged body. It was built to intimidate enemies and win friends. No terrorist with a sane mind would want to make this man an enemy. No woman would turn down a chance to make this man a friend.

He reached behind his back and retrieved a large automatic pistol. His expression a little coy, he nodded to her. "My stick."

"I can't remember when I've seen a bigger one."

"Oh, you probably say that to all the boys." He crossed the large kitchen to a peeling yellow door with an upper section of glass panes. He flicked the switch for the back-porch light and glanced out, the pistol grasped casually in his hand.

Betty watched him with reluctant fascination. He was so unlike any man she'd known before. Animal vitality radiated from him; he had a hard, dangerous look, but when he switched the light off and turned to wink at her, his face once again impressed her with the elegant strength in its lines. And his eyes, those light-green eyes, held both humor and unabashed sensuality.

"The microwave just buzzed," he told her.

"Oh." Feeling foolish, Betty pivoted and removed the mugs of water. She dumped instant hot chocolate into them from paper packets and stirred the mixture with a communal spoon. "Nothing fancy. If I could find my other spoon, I'd let you use it."

"Why are you living like this?"

Betty almost told him the truth. *Having invested most of my money in the early career of the next superstar of pop music, I am now broke.*

But she didn't need more humiliation in that area of her past, so she merely smiled and said, "I want to have several contractors bid on the remodeling job. There's no point in moving my things to the house until the work is finished."

"Why did you move in so early?"

"I was anxious to get my restaurant started in town. I have a lot of catering jobs scheduled during the next few weeks, too, so I'm trying to keep everything floating during the transition."

"What kind of catering jobs do you do?"

"Everything from family reunions to corporate parties. All casual. Barbecue is definitely a casual food. I've catered private picnics for the rich and infamous who have homes over on Lake Lanier, and I've catered public hoedowns for some of the state's biggest politicians."

"You have a big staff?"

"Nope." She handed him his mug. "Right now I have no staff at all. But I can handle the catering, except for the really big jobs, by myself. With barbecue, you just set it up, set it out, and keep the refills coming. You don't need much help serving the food."

"But what about the restaurant?"

"I've hired a manager for that. Andy Parsells. Do you know him?"

"You got Andy to leave the Hamburger Barn? He's been the head cook there as long as I can remember."

"He was making a crummy salary, and he had no medical benefits or pension. Plus he likes my reputation. He knows I'm headed for the big time."

"Hmmm. With a location in Webster Springs?"

"There's a lot of tourist traffic here because of the mountains and Lake Lanier." She sipped her hot chocolate and looked at him proudly. "People will drive up from Atlanta just to eat at my restaurant, because I'm

going to sell the best barbecue in this part of the country. And if they don't come to my restaurant, they'll at least buy my barbecue sauce, because I'm planning to market it. Eventually, I'll go national."

Max leaned against a cracked countertop and laid the gun down beside him. He cupped his mug, and his big hands swallowed it, made it look delicate. "You must have a damned good recipe for your barbecue sauce."

"You bet. There's nothing else like it. The recipe has been guarded by the Quint family for at least two generations. My grandfather, William, passed it along to my father. My father made it famous among our friends and neighbors. And he gave the recipe to me on my eighteenth birthday. When you taste it, you'll know you've never had anything better."

"I'm afraid not. *My* grandfather made the best barbecue sauce in the civilized world. I remember it from when I was a kid. People used to beg him to make it."

"Brag, brag, brag," she taunted mildly.

"Don't worry. The recipe was lost when he died. You're safe."

"My, oh, my," she deadpanned. "I can relax."

They were interrupted by the uneven thudding of Faux Paw's feet on the stairs. Several seconds later she ambled into the kitchen and stopped to eye Max curiously, her stubby tail twitching.

"Hello, mutant," he said pleasantly.

Betty knelt and stroked Faux Paw's head. "Ignore him, sweetie. Takes one to know one."

"Where did you get this creature—from a pet shop in the *Twilight Zone*?"

"My mother is on the board of directors at the Atlanta Humane Society. I've done a lot of volunteer work for the society myself. When Faux Paw's owner dumped her there, I was first in line to adopt her."

"Do I get the impression that you're part of the Atlanta blue blood scene?"

Betty stood, smiling sardonically. "I'm only blue-

blooded on Mother's side of the family. I'm a Quint on the other side, you know. Pioneer stock. Nouveau riche. My father made his money selling real estate to Yankees."

"Damn! A scalawag who sold the home place to carpetbaggers!"

She couldn't help laughing. "Not quite. He's a southern gentleman with a keen business mind, that's all. I inherited it, if I do say so myself."

"So what was it like growing up half blue-blooded and half nouveau riche?"

"Oh, just the usual. Vacations in Europe, season tickets to the symphony, weekends spent playing tennis at the club. I dated boys who had Roman numerals behind their last names."

"Boys with names like 'Snedley Beausquart the Fourth,' " Max said slyly.

"They weren't *that* pompous."

He crossed one ankle over the other and regarded her with half-shut eyes, making her feel so awkward that she lowered her gaze and pretended to study her mug. He chuckled softly. "So why haven't you done your duty and married a Snedley by now?"

"Most of the Snedleys were boring and narrowminded." She took a swallow from her mug, raised carefully guarded eyes to his, and said flatly, "So I caught myself a free-spirited musician. Or he caught me. I'm not sure which."

"Hmmm. You married him?"

"Oh, no. We were too cool to get married. At least he was. We had an . . . an understanding, you see. Unfortunately, I understood that one day we'd get married, and he understood that one day he'd get a recording contract and move to Los Angeles."

"Alone?"

"Oh, he asked me to come along. But I was tired of being a 'significant other.' I had started to feel like an awfully *insignificant* other." Betty kept her expression neutral, but feelings of resentment rose inside her again, directed at Max and his carefree attitude. "I spent a lot

of years telling myself that marriage didn't matter. Well, I was lying to myself. It does matter, at least to me."

Abruptly she shook her head and looked heavenward. "Aaagh! I'm spilling my guts to a man who thinks weddings are a joke!" She leveled a hard gaze at Max, daring him to deny it.

He didn't take the dare. "They are a joke."

"Why?"

"Because about half of all marriages end in divorce. Because a lot of people only get married out of loneliness, or because it makes sex convenient, or because their parents brainwashed them into believing that there's something wrong with them if they *don't* want to get married."

"You can't tell me that you've never loved a woman and thought that it would be nice to spend the rest of your life with her."

"You're right. But I can tell you that I've never seriously considered getting married. I live in the present. Marriage is based on fantasizing about the future."

"I bet a lot of women have left you, hmmm?"

He chuckled coldly. "In the marines I was transferred to a new base every two or three years. I did most of the leaving, whether I wanted to or not."

"You don't sound heartbroken."

"Sorry." He drained his hot chocolate and reached around her to set the mug on the counter. "How heartbroken are you over the musician? Deathless love should have made you follow him to L.A. Maybe you didn't love him as much as you think you did."

Betty straightened with ominous dignity. He was wrong, of course. "Don't foist your cynical attitudes on me."

"A little defensive, are you? A sign of inner turmoil. Uncertainty? A niggling intuition that I'm right?"

"It doesn't really matter what you think of my reasons. I moved here to start something new, something permanent. I'm not going to waste any more time on men who aren't interested in that." She half-turned and plunked her mug down on the counter.

"I'm permanent. I'm not going anywhere."

"Good. It'll be interesting to hear all the gossip about your romances. One day I'll tell my grandchildren that I knew you when you were young, and you haven't changed a bit. There's something to be said for creating that kind of legacy."

He had gone very still. Either he was angry, or he was calculating his next move. Regardless, his towering, silent scrutiny made her struggle to ignore the poignant mixture of regret and resentment in her chest.

"We'll see," he said softly.

Betty tried to laugh. It came out as a huffing, high-pitched, anxious sound, and she kicked herself mentally. She shook her head and looked at him pensively. "Why don't you and I call a truce and be friends? And I mean *just* friends. That way we won't keep on disappointing each other."

His dark expression lightened with amusement and speculation. "So you've been hoping for something from me? What is it? I hate to disappoint you."

She held up both hands. "Oh, no. You're not drawing me into a word game."

"I already have. But relax. Let's be friends." He came forward a few steps and held out his right hand. His eyes glimmered with laughter. "Shake?"

"You have more smooth moves than a greased snake."

"You should have been a drill sergeant. You've got a way with words. What are you afraid of—a simple handshake?"

She clasped his hand firmly. They shook. He stroked the center of her palm with his fingers as he drew away, and she cursed him silently because his touch made her breath shorten and her skin grow hot. Betty turned away, hoping that he couldn't read her reaction easily.

"More hot chocolate?" she muttered.

"No thanks. I've got an air mattress to inflate." He started to leave, then stopped so close that his thighs were almost, but not quite, brushing her hips. His

scent, a combination of leather, wool, and fresh autumn air, was distinctly masculine and provocative.

Betty stared at the mugs and didn't move. "I'll bring you a few blankets. Oh, there's plenty of wood if you want to start a fire and sleep in front of the fireplace."

"Thanks." His warm breath caressed her cheek. "You're being very nice to a man who makes you feel uncomfortable."

"I'm not uncomfortable," she said between gritted teeth as he left the kitchen. Alone, she bent over and, shaking her head in exasperation, covered her face with both hands. She felt as if she were on fire.

Several hours later Betty awoke with his voice in her ear and his hand on her shoulder. She knew something was wrong with the scenario, and after a second she realized what—he was in her bedroom, and she was in bed. She sputtered and tried to move away.

"Sssh, babe," he whispered, gently holding her still. "There's someone or something in your cellar. I want you to get dressed and stay by the phone. I'm going to check the cellar out."

"But there were *three* of those guys. What if—"

He laughed grimly. "They'd better be bad if there are only three."

She brushed a hand over her eyes and double-checked. Yes, he was for real. "Look, John Wayne, I don't want you to get hurt. I mean, if you get beat up or shot in my cellar, I'll feel obligated to be nice to you."

"Exactly. How about a smooch for the departing warrior?" He bent over her and took her mouth with a hard, caressing kiss, then trailed a finger over her lips. "I can die semi-happy now." Then he was gone, padding out of her bedroom and down the hall, walking so softly that his hiking boots were nearly soundless on the creaking wood floor.

She scooted out of bed and fumbled in a tall wicker basket where she had stored some of her clothes. Pull-

ing a pink jogging suit over her pajamas, she shoved her feet into loafers and tiptoed downstairs.

Faux Paw sat on a low step, attentive and curious. Betty stroked the cat's brindle head distractedly and hurried past. She was an orderly person, not given to cravings for adventure—except, she thought with disgust, where men were concerned. But she wouldn't spend any more years of her life on that craving. Even if Max Templeton had invaded her life and house and, apparently, had appointed himself her protector.

As she ran to the phone and stood listening intensely for any sound from the cellar, it occurred to her that her musician had never offered to protect her from anything more dangerous than bad vibes at a Grateful Dead concert.

The silence was a rough cloak that rubbed her nerves raw. She stood it as long as she could and then, her mouth acid with fear, she tiptoed through the kitchen and out the back door. Betty opened the screened door on the back porch and looked to the left, where one half of the cellar door stood open.

She returned to the kitchen, searched through one of her cardboard boxes, and pulled a carving knife from its wooden safety sheath. Like any serious cook, she kept her knives honed to a razor edge. With the carving knife clasped in her hand like a small sword, she headed back outdoors and went to the cellar. The pumping of her blood roared in her ears as she waited at the top of the steps.

"Max?" she called down softly. She called again and listened for a full minute, but there was no answer. What was he doing? Why hadn't he turned the lights on?

Call the sheriff, her typical, reasonable inner voice told her.

That won't do Max much good if he's already in trouble, a new, fiercer voice countered.

She descended into the dark cellar one heart-stopping step at a time. Its cold, clammy blackness made her

shiver. At the base of the narrow stairs she braced her feet apart and held the knife in front of herself with both hands as she tried to interpret shapes in the dark.

Samurai Betty, she thought, poking the air experimentally.

Her blood froze when a tiny trickle of dirt cascaded from the red-clay wall behind her. She started to pivot, but a heavy forearm circled her neck, and a hand grabbed both of her hands in a twisting grip that made her drop the knife.

"Oh, Max, you cretin," she said with relief and annoyance. "Stop it."

"Shut up."

It wasn't Max's voice.

Instant terror pumped adrenaline into her muscles. She brought her elbows back and jabbed her captor's ribs. Her heels beat a drumroll on his legs. The overhead light came on. Max loomed over both her and the stranger, his face composed in the deadly grimace of a wolf focusing on its prey.

He jammed the barrel of his gun into the face behind Betty. "One. Two—"

"All right, man, all right!"

Suddenly she was free. Max latched a hand onto her shoulder and jerked her out of the way, and after she bounced off the opposite clay wall, she swung around and looked at the scene numbly.

Max had pinned a brawny young man against the other wall. The man's jeans and denim jacket were covered in dirt and bits of leaves, and his sneakers were filthy. Either he'd been running through the woods, or he'd just come out of hibernation, Betty observed wryly.

He looked cross-eyed at the automatic pistol that was under his nose. He kept his hands plastered against the cellar wall behind him.

"Where are your two friends?" Max asked softly.

"I don't know. I swear. We got separated. Don't shoot me."

"Then don't even breathe wrong."

"I'm not breathing at all."

Betty found her voice. "I have some rope."

"Good." Max smiled coldly, his eyes never leaving the other man's. "Let's hang him."

She didn't believe what she said next. But Max provoked her to a giddy desire for mischief. "No, don't do that. I'll just go get the Dobermans."

The captive gasped. "No, lady. Please. I wasn't gonna hurt you! I was just trying to get past you and up the steps."

Max snuggled the gun barrel a little tighter against the man's upper lip. "Aw, he's kind of pitiful looking, babe. Why don't I just tie him up?"

"Oh, I suppose." She bent and retrieved the carving knife she'd dropped. "Darn. I didn't even get to nick him." She looked at the knife sadly. "Could I have a second chance?"

The captive moaned. "Please, lady."

"Oh, relax. I wouldn't cut off anything important."

"I'll talk her out of it. You better sit down," Max told him. "Slowly."

The man's knees buckled and he slid to the cellar floor, his face ashen. Betty took the gun that Max offered to her and aimed it at the man's head, smiling sweetly at him while Max got a coil of nylon rope from a nail on one of the cellar's support beams. Max quickly bound the man hands-to-feet.

"You scored fast on that calf tie, Tex," Betty noted in a twangy drawl.

Max tipped an imaginary Stetson to her. "Yup. Let's get the brandin' iron."

They left their nervous prisoner in the basement and went to the house, where she called the sheriff while Max padded through the downstairs rooms, making sure everything was secure. Within fifteen minutes her front yard filled with cars containing sheriff's deputies as well as police officers from the neighboring county. The other two robbery suspects had already been

caught. The third, spouting obscenities now that he felt safe, was hauled from Betty's cellar and taken away. After much interviewing, congratulations, and guffawing, everyone departed except, of course, Betty and Max.

They sat on the front-porch steps, wrapped in quilts. Dawn slipped through the meadow and forest around the house. The peacefulness of the autumn morning and the lingering undercurrent of shock made for a confusing mood. Betty huddled inside her quilt and began to shiver with fatigue and nerves.

"I've never shared anything like *this* with anyone else," she murmured. "I mean . . . the past night."

She turned to look at Max, emotions jumbled. There was a bond between them now, whether she wanted it or not. She fought it. He was the most distressing, most exciting man she'd ever met. And completely wrong for the path she'd planned for her life.

Beside her, his hips and thigh pressed companionably to hers, Max watched her with a quiet pleasure that made her feel even more unsettled. "We're great together," he said, his voice a deep purl. "I've never known a woman like you."

She wanted so badly to kiss him that the desire was an ache inside her throat. "Can a tiger ever change his stripes?" she asked in a small, tired voice.

He gave her a quizzical look, and then, as her meaning registered, his eyes clouded. "In other words, are my intentions honorable?"

"I know how prim the question sounds. I don't expect every man I meet to hand over a signed affidavit guaranteeing his interest in marriage." She searched his face desperately. "But with you I have a feeling that there wouldn't be any holding back. I'd be in over my head so fast that I wouldn't see the light until it blinded me. I want an affidavit."

He lifted a hand and cupped her chin. "I could lie to you, but I won't. I can't see myself ever getting married. After watching my father live happily by himself, and

after seeing so many of my Marine Corps cronies suffer through one divorce after another, I think the institution of marriage is highly overrated." He paused, looking at her somberly. "I may not believe in marriage, but I have nothing against love."

"What if you want children?"

"My career didn't give me much chance to put down roots, so I suppose that over the years I just lost interest in the possibility of having a family. I don't expect to have any children."

A cold, hard knot of disappointment settled inside her. "Thank you for being honest."

"Accept my honesty. Accept me." He bent his head close to hers and added gruffly, "Let's go inside the house. I'll make us both another cup of hot chocolate—with bourbon this time. When you're feeling warm and relaxed, I'll carry you up to your bedroom. I'll undress us both, and we'll curl up together under your electric blanket. And I promise you, you won't have any regrets about the way I make you feel."

For a moment her willpower shattered. She sagged against him and lifted her mouth to his, savoring the storm of sensation that kissing him produced even as a cry of resistance grew inside her chest. Betty brushed her lips over the tip of his nose, then his chin, his cheeks, his eyes. He bowed his head closer and shut his eyes, then sighed in a low, hoarse way that ignited her even more.

Shaking hard, she pulled back. "I can't, Max. I can't. Because I know what I want from life, just like you do, and neither of us is interested in compromise." She fought the knot in her throat and said miserably, "I moved here to forget one mistake. I won't start over with another one."

His troubled gaze held hers. A tinge of grim humor came into his eyes. "You're supposed to believe that you're the one woman who can change my mind about marriage."

She managed a small smile. "I believed that once

before about myself and a man. I was wrong. I'm not that irresistible."

Max frowned at her. He seemed emotionally intense, raw. Then he pulled her into his arms and kissed her until she was breathless and her mouth felt swollen. Holding her arms, he continued kissing her as he stood and brought her up with him.

Wobbling on the porch steps, her quilt falling to the ground unheeded, she kissed him back in a daze of greedy passion. But she began shaking her head. Half-crying, she backed away from him and held tight to the wooden balustrade beside the steps.

"You're irresistible in ways you never even considered," he told her hoarsely.

He tossed his quilt on the porch rail and walked into the house. Betty took deep breaths of crisp dawn air and touched her lips with a shaky hand. When he returned a minute later, he wore his wool poncho and carried his sleeping bag.

He passed her in silence but stopped at the base of the fieldstone steps. He looked up at her without anger in his eyes, although unhappiness made his expression hard. "Later," he said softly.

Betty watched him get into his Jeep. He tipped a hand to his forehead and gave her a small salute. She raised her hand in return, palm outward, but couldn't bring herself to wave good-bye.

Four

Values. In his dark, self-absorbed mood Max needed values that didn't need to be questioned. He shoveled the last bit of concrete mix around the base of the flagpole, then got down on his hands and knees and used a trowel to smooth the mix into a flat, circular pad.

Beyond the slope of his front yard the sun was setting over the forest and distant mountains, merging their reds and golds into the sky's soft purple. The air was pleasantly cool and smelled of wood smoke from Norma's chimney, hidden beyond the trees at the bottom of his driveway.

Ordinarily Max loved his privacy. One of the things he enjoyed most about Webster Springs was that here, only two miles from town, it was as if no town existed.

But this evening his thoughts were filled with Betty Quint, and loneliness lay in his stomach like a stone. He'd never felt this kind of craving for someone's company before, and he'd never wanted any other woman so badly.

"Straighten up. Stop moping," he ordered under his breath. "You were honest with yourself and with her. She was honest with you." He washed his hands in the spray from the hose that lay nearby, then dried them

on the tail of his sweatshirt and went to the Jeep, parked under an apple tree beside the house.

When he returned to the flagpole, he carried the carefully folded flag that his men had presented to him when he left the corps. He threaded it on the rope and ran it up the pole, then walked back a few paces and stood quietly, watching the evening wind lift the flag against the magenta sky.

He didn't regret his decision to leave the marines, because he'd begun to look at himself in the mirror and see a crusty leatherneck who had nothing permanent or meaningful in his life except the corps. But he was proud of his career. He had believed in the good of his work, the good of his country. He still did.

Max snapped to attention and saluted the flag. Then, because the sun had nearly disappeared and a bright-orange harvest moon would soon be rising, he quickly lowered the flag.

Frowning a little, he carried it across the lawn to a wooden bench under a grape arbor. As he sat down and began folding it he wondered if Betty would think he was corny and maudlin.

No, the lady believed in traditional values, he reminded himself. Home and hearth. God, country, and marriage. Marriage. He leaned back and shut his eyes, smiling grimly. He wasn't afraid of many things, but marriage was near the top of the list. He'd seen it break too many strong men. In a way, it had broken his father, because no woman had ever been able to replace Max's mother. His father had told him so, more than once.

But what if he never stopped wanting Betty Quint? How could he see her around town and resist an urge to seduce her by any means, fair or foul? Max groaned in bitter amusement and rubbed his forehead. He'd met her only four days ago, and yet here he sat, wrestling with his conscience, his libido, and a deep, growing sense that he'd never forgive himself if he let her get away.

This was worse than marriage.

Betty checked her bank balance. Dismayed, she checked it again. The bank machine patiently ground out another receipt while she gripped the steering wheel of her economy-model van. She grabbed the new receipt and inhaled sharply as it confirmed what the first one had said.

After a moment she slowly tucked the receipt into her leather purse, muttering under her breath, "That's what you get for being a fool, Betty Belle." The man in the cattle truck behind her honked his horn impatiently. She waved and quickly guided the van out of the drive-through and onto Main Street.

As she drove past handsome old one-story buildings that housed clothing boutiques, craft shops, and cafés, she propped an elbow on the window casing and leaned her head on one fist, tired and lost in plans. A block further she entered the town square, circled the stately courthouse that was now an arts center and museum for mountain crafts, then pulled down a side street to a restored Victorian-era cottage painted blue with white trim.

Betty parked at the curb for a moment and watched workmen set the restaurant sign into postholes they'd dug among the azaleas by the front walk. It was a handsome wooden sign painted blue to match the house, with the restaurant's name set in large, scrolling white letters. *Betty's Restaurant.*

She laughed despite the lump in her throat. You couldn't get more simple than that, and she liked it. It sounded friendly and unpretentious, while the house looked more formal. That was the combination she'd wanted, not as casual as most barbecue restaurants, but a home-style place at heart.

She drove around back and entered a graveled lot shaded by hickory trees. The trees had been a good-

luck sign, she'd thought when she'd bought the house. Her barbecue was hickory smoked. But good luck seemed to be fleeing as fast as the bank's computer could register her debits.

Her stomach in knots, she parked near the newly installed trash dumpster and sat with a pad and pen, working out her finances.

Max Templeton entered her mind, as he had so many times over the past few days. She could imagine his amazement if he knew just how little money she had. Would he be sympathetic or grimly amused at the idea?

Poor little rich girl. She'd spent years throwing away her time and money on a struggling musician, and now she was struggling along on a business loan and a dwindling savings account.

No, Max would be sympathetic, she thought dully. He'd probably offer her a strong shoulder, an attentive ear—and a lot of other body parts that she'd have trouble resisting.

She set her jaw and made some calculations. She'd drive down to the storage warehouse in Atlanta and gather a few of the furnishings that she'd moved from her condo and sell them.

The one thing she would *not* do was ask her parents for a loan. Her father would remind her that she'd gotten herself in this fix by foolishly spending five years as the girlfriend and sole support of Sloan Richards, needy musical genius.

Now, without anyone's help, she was gong to recover her dignity. She reached into a box on the passenger seat, lifted a bottle of thick red barbecue sauce, and gazed grimly at the homemade blue-and-white label. *Betty's Barbecue Sauce.* Simple name. Incredible taste. The key to financial success.

Men. Who needed them? In particular, Max Templeton. Who needed *him*? She put the bottle back distractedly and sighed. Some questions were best left unanswered.

• • •

Every October the chamber of commerce held its charity auction and dinner dance. Looking around the big, rustic room of the local winery, Betty felt more at home than she ever had at any of Atlanta's charity galas.

It had been a week since the emotional night with Max at her house, and she'd promised herself that she wouldn't look for him tonight. But she knew he'd been invited, and she glanced repeatedly toward the double doors at the far side of the room, where people were entering.

Despite every rebuking thought she directed at herself, her heart beat fast with anticipation. She made herself study the scenery.

This winery, set in a lush mountain valley, was hardly like its classical equivalents in France. The main building was a two-story country inn with lots of gray stone and hand-hewn timbers. This room was filled with primitive antiques, and the walls were hung with quilts. The pegboard floor was dotted with round braided rugs, and the giant fireplace hearth was decorated with pumpkins and bundles of cornstalks.

A trio of bearded men stood in one corner playing old folk tunes on a dulcimer, fiddle, and guitar. The banquet tables were set with handmade stoneware goblets and pewter utensils; a candlelit jack-o'-lantern grinned in the center of each table.

Betty swirled her glass of muscadine wine and glanced around the banquet table at her fellow diners. The men wore nice suits and the women pretty gowns, but Betty knew they'd have been the object of polite ridicule in her old circles, where no man was well dressed unless he owned at least one custom-made tuxedo and no woman would have been caught dead wearing a gown that had come from a department store rack.

"Quaint crew, aren't they?" her date whispered in her ear.

Betty twisted to look at Jay Steinberg, a friend she'd known since they were both chubby, braces-wearing nerds at an exclusive private high school. Jay was tall, lean, and handsome in an offbeat sort of way, with thick black hair and, despite his orthodontic history, an intriguing gap between his front teeth. He wore his Armani suit with perfect style. His tie was silk; his wristwatch, Cartier. He had already been made a full partner in an Atlanta architecture firm.

"They're all very nice," she said, frowning a little as she tried to remember whether Jay had always had a condescending air about him.

"Oh, I'm not putting them down. It's fascinating to see how the rural middle class lives."

She bent close to his ear and whispered, "Oh, yes! If you look closely, you'll see them do odd, puzzling things—like eat dinner, laugh, talk, and enjoy themselves."

Jay chortled and pressed a kiss to her cheek. "Betty, you're being a crab. I drove all the way up here from Atlanta just to be your escort. The least you can do is indulge my sense of humor."

Betty sat back, took a swallow of wine, and wished that the appetizer would arrive so that Jay would have something to do with his mouth besides talk. Her gaze darted to the double doors at the end of the room.

Max was looking straight at her.

He was also looking at Jay. He didn't look happy, though he should have, since a statuesque redhead in a tight black dress was holding his hand.

He idly stroked the lapel of his jacket aside and lifted a gold watch from a pocket on his vest. Whether custom-made or not, his black pinstripe suit fit his powerful body to perfection. Apparently, black string ties were his trademark, because he wore one again now.

Betty knew she should look away, should just nod and feign a casual greeting, but all she could do was stare at him.

He seemed to be having the same problem with her. The redhead, whom Betty dimly recalled having seen behind the counter of a bakery in town, was tugging on his hand and pointing to a banquet table where people were waving to them. Finally he blinked, returned the watch to his vest pocket, gave Betty a courteous smile with a hard edge to it, and accompanied his date to their table.

"Now *that* man has style," Jay commented, craning his head. "And she's incredible."

Betty fiddled with her napkin and rearranged her forks. When unnerved, she distracted herself with details. Once, after an argument with Sloan, she'd cleaned all the windows on the converted school bus she used on her catering jobs. Now she began polishing her knife.

Jay knew her too well. "Oh, Betty, I'm so rude," he apologized. "Forgive me."

"For ogling the redhead?" She patted his arm. "Go ahead. I was the one who introduced you to your first serious girlfriend, remember?"

"You're a doll. Do you know the redhead?"

"No." She thunked her knife down. She wasn't going near Max and his date, not even for Jay's benefit.

Jay looked forlorn. "Her friend looks like Clint Eastwood in a bad mood. I guess I better corral my lecherous thoughts."

"I'd put them in a deep freeze if I were you. I know Clint, and he's the type who'll twist your nose off if you make a pass at his lady."

"Ouch. You sound proud of him."

"Something like that."

When the shrimp cocktails arrived, she tried to keep her gaze on her plate. Invisible magnets seemed to pull her eyes toward Max. Finally she couldn't bear the intrigue and looked up. Max was taking a sip from his goblet, his head tilted toward the conversation of Grace Larson and her husband Ernie, the mayor.

Betty felt a poignant stab of disappointment, then chided herself for thinking that Max would be watching her. She muttered to herself and finally pivoted toward Jay. "Kiss me, you fool," she ordered.

He stopped a shrimp halfway to his mouth. "What?"

"Give me a semi-serious kiss on the lips."

"Are we trying to make someone jealous?"

"No, we're just trying to make me come back to reality."

"Betty Belle, this isn't a pep rally," he teased gently, "and you're not the plump ninth grader who wanted to show everyone that you were sexy enough to get a date, even it was with another plump ninth grader."

"But you're going to oblige me now, as you did then. Because you're my pal."

"Okay. Open your mouth."

"We're not trying for that much reality, Jay."

"I'm going to feed you my shrimp, darling."

"Oh. Good move."

Smiling, he slid his shrimp between her lips, then took her face between his hands and kissed her before she finished chewing. He sat back and looked satisfied. "*Now* will you introduce me to the redhead?"

"No. But thanks for the shrimp."

She sighed wearily and glanced toward Max. He wasn't at his table anymore. He was headed toward hers. He gracefully threaded through the tables in between, apparently guided by an athlete's sixth sense, because he never took a misstep despite the fact that his eyes remained on her the whole way.

She couldn't tell if their expression was angry, amused, or merely intense. She only knew that her body was rigid with dread and excitement.

He reached the table and clamped his hand on the back of her chair with a force that sent a small shiver through the chair and her. "How are you this evening, Betty?"

"Fine. And you?"

"Terrific."

She stared up at him a second, inhaling the light scent of his cologne, wondering if the air was crackling between them or if her nerves had been strained too far. A lifetime of formal training in etiquette made her swivel toward Jay. "Jay, I'd like to introduce you to Max Templeton, judge of the magistrate court in this county." She swiveled toward Max. "Max, I'd like to introduce you to Jay Steinberg, an old and very dear friend of mine from Atlanta."

"Pleased, I'm sure," Jay said, and rose to shake hands.

"Quite pleased," Max countered, sounding suspiciously prim.

They shook. Max looked down at her. "I have some business to discuss with you. Would you mind walking outside with me for just a moment?"

Trouble, her good sense warned. *Go,* everything else urged. "Of course. Please excuse us for a moment, Jay."

"Certainly. It was nice meeting you, Mr. Templeton."

Max smiled at him. "It was nice meeting you, Mr. Steinberg. I'll bring Betty back in a moment."

He took her arm as she stood, and propelled her out a side door so quickly that the flowing silk skirt of her russet-and-black gown threatened to become trapped between her legs.

They entered a deserted hallway and stopped under the softly filtered light of a stained-glass wall fixture. He faced her, and the intensity in his eyes was a secret no longer.

"A moment," she whispered with a note of warning. She felt as if she was swaying toward him, the magnets pulling at her whole body. "What did you want to discuss?"

"Just this—if you want to be kissed in public, come to me." He put his arms around her waist and pulled her upward so that she stood on her toes, teetering against him and grasping his shoulders for support.

"Max. Max . . ." she said desperately, shaking her head.

"I love your voice. Say my name again."

"*Maximilian,* don't—"

"Damned good." He kissed her, backing her against a soft quilt hanging on the wall. Betty struggled with her emotions for the length of time his hot, deliciously insistent mouth took to turn her into a conspirator. About two seconds.

She forgave herself for surrendering. He had a way of curling the tip of his tongue along the edge of her upper lip that no woman could resist. She quivered from the inside out, and a sweet, heavy feeling settled in her belly.

He brought a raw power to her that she'd never felt before; he didn't treat her roughly in the least, but she wanted to struggle within his arms and provoke the same struggle from him. She slid her hands down his torso and he shifted to let her grip the sides of his waist.

There was great gentleness in him, in the careful, responsive movements of his mouth and tongue, in the knowing way his hands slid up and down her back, lingering at the top each time to rub her shoulders above the gown's scooped neck. He had trapped her, but he wasn't forcing her.

Dazed, Betty rubbed circles with her palms at the sides of his waist and vaguely realized that she was pulling his hips closer. He was a big, solid man; his thighs felt like pillars of stone as they pressed closer, molding his lower body to hers in the most tantalizing way.

She drew her head back and looked at him groggily. He moved against her with a slow, grinding rhythm that made her bite her lower lip to keep from moaning.

"We'll go back inside and sit down with our respective dates as if nothing unusual has happened," he

commanded mildly, his voice very low and coaxing. He continued to caress her with slight flexing movements of his body. "We'll share a dance or two after the auction. We'll very politely leave with our dates at the end of the evening."

He paused, one honey-brown eyebrow arching wickedly. "Then we'll tell each of them some very polite reason why they have to go home, and we'll rendezvous at your place."

He stroked his hands up her back and brought them to rest at the base of her head, his thumbs caressing the tender skin beneath her topaz earrings as he pulled her closer. "And then we'll finish what we've started here. We'll finish it repeatedly, all night. In every way that pleases you. Until all you have the energy to do is put your head on my shoulder and fall asleep."

The breath shuddered out of her in a long sigh. The images he had just painted made her legs weak, and she wondered how she'd stand without his strength and passion.

The thought had unsettling implications. She had to stand alone, especially where Max was concerned. She'd known when she'd returned his kiss that it would only be a temporary indulgence, a sample of a glorious meal— but only a sample—for a starving woman.

"Your . . . date," she said slowly, her lips heavy from sensation. "She would have been in your bed tonight; she *will be* in your bed tonight if you're not with me."

"No." His gaze held hers with almost fierce defense. "There hasn't been anyone else since I met you. There wouldn't have been anyone tonight."

"Max, don't—"

"You sounded disappointed at the idea that I might take someone else to bed, but you don't want to hear that I'm *not* taking anyone to bed because of you. Can't you believe that I'm capable of being faithful, that I'm not promiscuous? I'm not interested in sleeping around. I want you, only you."

"For now, you mean. For tonight, and if we were happy after that, then for as long as we enjoyed each other's company, on your terms."

"Can't we just start with *tonight,* babe? Do you really want to stand here in the hall and plan the rest of our lives?"

She forced her hands up to his shoulders and made them rest there lightly. "No, I don't want to plan the rest of our lives," she said with strained control, "but I don't want to lie to myself." She searched his eyes, and let him see all the sorrow and vulnerability in hers. "I already know that I could . . . love you. And I already know what I'd be hoping for if I did. And I know that it wouldn't be what you'd want. And I have a feeling that I'd eventually be hurt in a way that would make the other time seem pleasant."

"With the musician," he said flatly.

"Yes."

"But you won't—"

"No. I won't."

"I predict that you will. You *will* change your mind. Because we need to be together, and everything else is going to take care of itself."

She raised her chin and eyed him bitterly. "Oh? How will everything take care of itself? Will you and Hugh Hefner trade brain cells? Even *he* got married."

Max stepped back from her but lifted his hands to her ruffled hair and stroked it into place. He smiled thinly. "Thank you for taking a moment to discuss business with me, Betty. I won't keep you from your dinner any longer. I might suggest that before you return to Mr. Steinberg, you venture to the ladies' lounge and check your lipstick."

"I don't have to. You're wearing it."

"Indeed. You're an animal." He reached inside his jacket and retrieved a handkerchief. Wiping his mouth slowly, he nodded to her. "I look forward to discussing business with you again, soon."

When she returned to her chair, Jay asked slyly, "Are you in trouble with the law?"

"Nothing I can't settle out of court." Betty tracked Max's course through the crowded room as he returned to his table. "I think it'll be safe for you to chase the redhead of your dreams tonight. I'll make sure that Max introduces you to her."

"Oh? And what brought about this change of heart?"

"Don't look a gift horse in the mouth."

He whinnied softly and pawed the table with one fist.

After dinner the auction began, with the stout, pink-faced Ernie Larson as auctioneer. Before each bid the contributing merchant was asked to come up and describe what she or he had donated.

There was a varied offering of finely made crafts, paintings, books, furniture, clothes, jewelry, and food. Eventually Ernie introduced the redhead as co-owner of the Taste of Honey Bakery. Her name was Ann. She came to the microphone in the front of the room and smiled broadly, then in a voice as sweet as pecan pie said that her donation was a fifty-dollar gift certificate for baked goods.

"What am I bid?" Ernie boomed.

Betty saw Max start to raise his hand. She supposed that a gentleman ought to bid on his date's donation, but it made her less happy. Despite his gallant words in the hall, he was the kind of man who could have a different woman on his arm every week if he wanted. And he probably wanted. She wasn't going to forget that.

Jay leapt to his feet. "Two hundred dollars!"

Everyone swiveled to stare at him. Betty saw Max lower his hand, give Jay a thoughtful look, then smile. He caught her eye and lifted a brow in droll challenge. *That takes care of my date's attention.*

It certainly did, because now Ann looked at Jay in utter delight, her hands clasped over her heart. After a shocked Ernie determined that no one wanted to bid

more than two hundred dollars for a fifty-dollar gift certificate, he whacked his gavel on the auction podium. "Sold!"

Ann ogled Jay all the way back to her table. He blew her a kiss and, smiling grandly, sat down. "Slick. I'm slick."

"I was going to ask you to bid on me, you rake."

"Oops. I just spent most of my mad money, but I'll make a valiant effort. Why?"

"Because I suspect that Max Templeton—"

"And next," Ernie called, "is the newest member of our chamber of commerce, the owner of a restaurant that'll be opening soon on Spencer Street. Betty Quint, come on up."

Betty pushed her chair back and sighed. Across the room Max rose a little, turned his chair to face the microphone squarely, then sat down on the edge with all the confident anticipation of an art dealer about to spend millions on a Picasso.

"It's hopeless," she muttered. "I'm about to be sold to a man who wants a barbecue-catering love slave."

At the microphone she put on a happy smile and avoided looking at him. He sat only about a dozen feet away. "Good evening," she said to the audience pleasantly. "My restaurant will be opening in about two weeks. Because I'm better at cooking than at making up names, it will simply be called 'Betty's Restaurant.'"

She paused, clasping her hands in front of her. Her palms were sweaty. "My specialty is barbecue. I've been a barbecue caterer for six years, and now I'm going to expand into the restaurant business. Tonight I'm donating a catered barbecue dinner for twenty people. All the winning bidder has to do is tell me where and when, and I'll provide everything. Thank you."

"All right," Ernie boomed, waving his gavel. "What am I bid— "

"One hundred dollars!" Jay called from the back.

"One hundred and ten!" another man yelled. Betty

darted a look at the man and cringed inside. Claymore Perkins lolled back in his chair and smirked at her over the cigarette in his lips. Claymore owned the local pawn and salvage shop, where he displayed his collection of Elvis portraits on velvet. Claymore had already asked her for a date several times, and he'd gotten sarcastic after the most recent of her diplomatic refusals. She had nothing against his work, but his attitude was sleazy.

"One hundred and twenty!" Jay countered, but he didn't sound as enthusiastic this time.

"One hundred and thirty," Claymore said immediately, his cigarette bobbing. "I got a taste for some of your sauce."

"One hundred and thirty . . . five," Jay grumbled.

"One-fifty," Claymore retorted.

Jay shook his head and gave Betty an apologetic look. Her dread increased, as well as her absurd disappointment toward Max. His lack of interest hurt her feelings even as she kicked herself for caring.

"Anymore?" Ernie asked, glancing around the room.

Betty refused to look at Max, but realized that she was grinding her teeth. She rebuked herself for being so certain that he'd make a grand gesture just to pursue her. *You aren't exactly a femme fatale, my dear. And didn't you want him to leave you alone?*

"Going once," Ernie said, raising his gavel. "Going twice."

She bit the inside of her cheek. She'd never speak to Maximilian Templeton again.

"Going—what? What's that, Max?"

Her mouth dry, Betty jerked her gaze to Max. He was holding up his hand, palm forward, fingers and thumb spread. A knowing, wicked smile curved his mouth, and he studied her through narrowed eyes. "Five hundred," he called softly, his voice so rich and full that it carried through the room regardless.

Everyone gasped. Betty looked at him shrewdly. His smile grew smug. He had not only bought her time and

attention, but he'd let her squirm first, just to show that he had the upper hand.

"Claymore, are you done?" Ernie inquired.

Claymore grunted, looking disgusted. "Yeah."

"Sold!" Ernie rapped the gavel. "A catered barbecue dinner for twenty people, to Max Templeton. Thank you, Max. Thank you, Betty."

She swiveled woodenly and nodded to Ernie. "It was my pleasure." Then she left the microphone and glided regally past Max, ignoring him, trying not to clench her fists.

"Later, babe," he said with challenge in his voice as she swept by. "My mouth is watering already."

Five

Max tracked her down on Monday as she was hanging lace curtains over the windows in the restaurant's main room. "Here comes the judge," Andy Parsells announced.

Standing on a stepladder, she glanced hurriedly over her shoulder. Max stood in the double doorway to the house's central hallway. His hands were shoved into the pockets of handsome gray slacks. From his polished loafers to his white windbreaker and crisp white shirt, he was dressed for a laid-back business day as a rural magistrate. He wore his string tie, of course.

"Thanks, Andy," she said distractedly, nodding to her manger as a signal that he could leave.

Andy headed back to the kitchen, where he was unpacking utensils and pots. He was short and rotund, with a bulbous nose and a head full of cantankerous gray hair. In clothing he was strictly a biker type—faded jeans, a white T-shirt with a pack of cigarettes rolled into one sleeve, black boots, and a black jacket. It was hard to imagine him as a grandfather of seven and a deacon in one of the local churches, which he was.

He was also a master at running a restaurant. He'd already lined up a dependable, mature staff of kitchen workers and servers. Betty knew that her good wages

had helped him acquire them, but also they'd wanted to work for Andy, who'd developed a fine reputation as the Hamburger Barn's head cook.

"Getting him was quite a coup," Max commented, walking toward her. "I wouldn't have believed that he'd work for a woman."

"He was a tough cookie. When we were negotiating, he went along on one of my catering jobs and saw how I ran my business. I think he was impressed that I toted and fetched alongside my employees. He said I wasn't a snob."

A long swath of lace hung over Betty's left shoulder. She swept the tail of it around her neck and posed like a grande dame, one hand on her jutted hip. "Do you feel threatened by women in power?"

Max stopped at the base of her ladder and looked up at her slyly. "Only if they demand a rate increase on my electric bill . . . Oh, you mean women in *power*."

"Cute, Maximilian."

"I approve. I like the new order of things. There are fewer games." He sighed dramatically. "Or different games, at least."

She took her time coming down from the ladder, fiddling with the curtain draped across the front of her long-sleeved T-shirt. Then, feeling awkward in his presence, and to emulate his cocky, casual attitude, she stuck her hands in the front pockets of her jeans.

The slit-eyed appraisal Max gave every inch of her was hard on her nerves. She rocked back and forth on her heels, eyeing him with all the nonchalance she could muster. "Sorry I missed the dancing on Saturday night. My escort had to leave early. He had a long drive back to Atlanta."

"Poor guy. Then he made the long drive *back* here on Sunday, so he could spend the day with Ann."

"He *what*? He did?"

"Hmmm. I saw them having lunch together at the deli."

She recovered her composure a little. "Well, that's nice. I hope they enjoyed each other's company."

"You're chicken-livered, Betty. You should have stayed and danced with me Saturday night."

"I have a tough liver, thank you. I know how to avoid trouble too. I don't dance with men who are manipulative and devious."

He dismissed her complaint with a lazy wave of one hand. "I'm here to schedule my catered barbecue dinner. Instead of one shindig for twenty people, I'd like ten dinners for two people. You and me."

"It doesn't work that way."

"For five-hundred dollars, it ought to."

"You probably could have had me at your beck and call for no more than two hundred. Claymore Perkins isn't an extravagant man—except where his velvet paintings of Elvis are concerned."

"So I have you at my beck and call? I like that way of putting it."

She shifted impatiently. "When do you want your party? I'm booked up for the next few Saturdays. I haven't done much catering lately because I've been busy here, but that's about to change. People around the lake have lots of parties at this time of year because the mountains are so pretty. They invite all their friends up."

"Do you do any catering on weekdays?"

"Certainly."

"How much advance notice do you need?"

"For a small group, one day."

"I can have you at my beck and call tomorrow then?"

She thought for a moment. She'd have to go down to her folk's house in Atlanta and get the bus this evening, then spend all day tomorrow preparing food. Well, she'd been planning to move the bus up here this week, anyway. And it would be best to get the ordeal with Max over with as soon as possible.

"Tomorrow is fine. Can you actually get nineteen

friends together on such short notice? Are there nine-teen people around here who can put up with you?"

"I'll just pare down the list of my old girlfriends. Pick the top fifty and draw names." He chuckled dryly at the deadpan look she gave him. "Actually, I'm going to give my prize to a couple of people who are getting married tomorrow night. I want you to cater their reception."

Her double take made him sigh. "See? I'm not such a jackass. They're elderly and they don't have much money. A widow and a widower marrying for the second time. Their friends from the senior center are all invited, and they were going to have a reception with cheap cookies and punch. If you'll provide the barbecue, I'll provide a wedding cake."

"All right." She was surprised and once again thrown off balance. "What time?"

"Seven."

"Okay."

Around Max her emotions had a disturbing way of flip-flopping. Now she wanted to just gaze at him in melting wonder. He looked down at her with a somber, troubled expression. Neither of them moved, but she felt as if they'd stepped closer. She realized after several seconds that her lips were parted and that she was, indeed, staring at him in wonder.

"I'll see you at six," she mumbled, lost in his eyes. "You're a nice boy, Maximilian. Always full of surprises."

"I can be incredibly good. Better than your wildest dreams."

"And so humble."

"See you tomorrow. At six."

After he strolled out, she got her hypnotized muscles in gear and followed quickly to the veranda's screened door, so that she could watch him. He descended the steps and went down the walkway without looking back, but when he reached the street, where he'd parked his Jeep, he turned and saw her in the doorway.

"You're beautiful in lace and denim," he called gruffly.

She touched the curtain hanging across her breasts.

By the time he drove away, she'd succumbed to a long, yearning sigh, and wished desperately that she had stayed to dance with him at the chamber of commerce party, where it might have been safe to indulge a little.

Max paced the small foyer outside the wedding parlor, his long black coat shoved back behind his hands which he'd sunk into his trouser pockets. Norma came out of the parlor, unfastening the buttons of the white sweater she'd donned over her considerable bosom and blue dress. She considered the dress, with a tiny heart embroidered beneath its lace collar, her work uniform.

"It was chilly in the parlor. I turned up the furnace so the old folks won't get the shivers," she noted, eyeing Max curiously. "What's wrong with you, son?"

"I'm just wondering where the barbecue queen is. It's six-fifteen. How can she set up food for twenty people by seven o'clock?"

"It's not like you to fidget."

He halted and frowned in thought. "I know. Dammit, I'm acting like a fool."

"Are you worried about the food or Betty?"

"I'm not *worried* about her, I'm—"

"I heard she's set on finding a husband and thinks you and your bachelor ways are bad news."

Exasperated, he coyly wagged a finger at Norma. "It's not nice to listen to gossip. Especially when it's true."

"What are you goin' to do about that truth?"

"Change her mind."

Norma crossed her arms over her chest. "Sweet talk the lady? Even if she's off limits?"

"She's not off limits."

"If she's the marrying kind and you're not, you ought to let her alone. Or overhaul your ideas about marriage, so you won't end up like your daddy."

"Pa never needed a marriage license to be happy."

"He wasn't happy. He put on a big show whenever you were visitin', telling you how many lady friends he

had, but he was lonely a lot of the time, and he told me more than once that he envied old folks who had a wife or husband. And he wished he had more children, and grandchildren too."

Max stared at her in disbelief. "No. He could have remarried if he'd felt that way."

Norma shook her head. "He waited too long. Nobody'd have him. His reputation was too scary. See, lots of ladies invited the old tomcat home for a little cater-wauling, but none of them wanted to keep him."

Max studied the blunt honesty in her serious brown eyes, and his astonishment gave way to dull sorrow on his father's behalf. So Pa hadn't been as carefree as he'd wanted everyone to think. Max gritted his teeth. That still didn't mean he would have been happier married.

"I'm not my father. I'm going to have someone important in my life, someone I love and who loves me. But I'm not going to pledge all the impossible promises in a marriage vow to another human being. Two people shouldn't have to promise the world to each other. That only leads to disappointment."

"You won't have much of a 'someone' then. And you sure won't have Miss Betty Quint, because from what I've heard, she wouldn't put up with second best."

Max knew when he'd lost a debate with Norma. He bit back his frustration and released it on the foyer's flowery carpet and wallpaper. "Dammit! This room is so old looking, dinosaurs must have squatted in it. I'm gong to have it redone."

"You forgettin', Maximilian? Your Pa left this place to *me*. Don't you go rantin' and ravin' about my perfectly fine foyer just because you're mad at your old cynical self."

He threw up his hands. "I'm not mad at . . . I wish Betty would get here!"

"Calm down. I see headlights turning off the road."

Max swung the front door open so hard that he shook the beveled-glass insert. Lumbering into the small

graveled parking area beyond the house's lawn was a remodeled school bus, painted silver. "Betty's Barbecue" was scrolled on the side in large maroon letters.

Betty honked the horn at him and brought the bus to a stop. Crossing the lawn with long, angry steps, Max arrived in the parking lot just as she cranked the door open.

"You look worried," she commented, peering at him from the driver's seat. She looked calm, neat, and gorgeous in slim black trousers and a gold sweater, with lacquered black-and-gold combs pulling her hair back from her face.

"You're late," he announced sharply.

She drew back, obviously startled. "I said six o'clock."

"It's six-twenty."

"That's still more than enough time."

"And you're not exactly dressed to work."

"I'll put a big white chef's apron over my clothes. What should a barbecue caterer wear—overalls, a straw hat, and a name tag that says, 'Hi, I'm Betty. Enjoy my pork butts'?"

"All right, all right, never mind."

He leapt onto the bottom steps and glanced impatiently around the bus's interior. What he saw startled him. The back half of the bus had been converted into a restaurant-quality kitchen.

But in the front half of the bus were windows covered in chintz curtains. Behind the driver's seat was a small booth with a table that bore a checkered cloth. The effect was warm and inviting.

"This is the first time I've ever had the diner delivered along with the dinner," Max told her.

Betty flicked a switch, and the bus filled with light from large fluorescent fixtures in the ceiling. "Clear out of my way, Major," she said firmly. "I'm about to charge."

"Now you're panicking about the lack of time."

"No, I've been doing this work for years, and I'm a professional. I know exactly how much time I need to set up the food." She unbuckled her seat belt and

tossed it aside, frowning at him as she did. "Why are you angry with me?"

"I think you need to be more punctual."

"I think you woke up on the wrong side of the fox-hole this morning. You're in a terrible mood."

He jerked a thumb toward the house. "Just haul your tail. Hand me something to carry inside."

She stood slowly, put her hands on her hips, and met his eyes with a look of dangerous intensity. "I can handle this alone. Scram."

He climbed the steps and planted himself in front of her. She threw her head back and silently defied him, a challenging, stubborn expression on her face.

"I spent five-hundred dollars. I bought your services for this shindig," he said between clenched teeth. "I'm in charge."

He was standing so close to her that he could smell the rose scent of her perfume and see the charcoal shadow that accented her gray eyes. Now that gray turned as dark as a thundercloud. "This is my ship, and I'm the captain. You're about to be thrown overboard."

"Why are you refusing my offer of help?"

"Because you're not offering, you're ordering. I don't respond very well to the whims of authority. That's why I've always preferred to be my own boss."

"I think that you hate like hell to be anywhere near me, and you waited until the last minute to come here."

She hesitated, her eyes searching his. Then she said softly, "You're right."

Tense silence hung between them. Taken aback, he said finally, "You'd never make it as a diplomat."

"Every time I'm near you, I feel as if I'm walking a tightrope. I'm terrified that I might fall. And you enjoy making me feel that way. Why should I want to be around you under those circumstances?"

"Let yourself fall. I'll catch you."

"*Please*, could we drop this subject? I have work to do."

He glared down at her, but she didn't budge. Elemental warnings ran through him—desire and respect and a deep, compelling decision to get her into his bed soon, no matter how he had to do it. He didn't need marriage, but he did need her—more than he wanted to admit at the moment.

"I'll go if you agree to one request," he told her. "I want you to serve *my* barbecue to me at my house, after the wedding reception. And I want you to eat dinner with me."

She nodded primly. "All right. If no more than eighteen people attend the wedding, you'll have two dinners left. But if twenty people show up, I'll serve you diddly squat."

"Great. Put some extra sauce on my diddly." He shook his head. "There won't be more than eighteen people."

"How do you know?"

"Because I called the bride-to-be and asked her."

"You really like to plan your moves, don't you?"

"I plan for every possibility and stay alert for any sign of vulnerability in the opposing force's defenses."

"What if your operation fails?"

"Then I resort to Plan B."

"What's that?"

He merely smiled, tipped his hand to his forehead in a salute to a valiant foe, then pivoted and left the bus. He didn't know Plan B himself, but there had to be one.

Betty ducked into the back of the parlor for just a minute after her preparations were finished in the next room. Irma Bryson, seventy-nine, and Lawrence Kent, seventy-five, were married in a quiet, pretty little ceremony that left Betty in more turmoil.

The sight of wispy Irma clutching a bouquet of carnations against her purple dress and stalwart Lawrence clutching Irma's hand against the jacket of his old blue suit filled her with poignant happiness. The

sight of Max gently and solemnly marrying the elderly couple filled her with confused tenderness. How could this man, with his deep capacity for caring, reject the ultimate expression of it for himself?

She left the parlor and went to the reception room, where her heated serving trays were lined up neatly on a long banquet table that paralleled one wall. Handsome straight-backed chairs lined the opposite walls. The polished pine floor was dotted with beautiful old rugs. Opaque white wall sconces filtered light upward, and a chandelier of dewdrop crystals hung from the high ceiling.

The room offered old-fashioned dignity. Max offered modern convenience. Was there a middle ground where they could meet? She went behind the serving table and poked aimlessly at a pan of chopped barbecue chicken.

She studied the punch bowl that sat on a separate table near the end of the barbecue line. Next to the bowl was a magnificent two-tiered sheet cake covered in pink roses and inscribed "Irma and Lawrence—Much Happiness."

Betty admired Max's taste in wedding cakes. He was both generous and kind.

"Smells wonderful!" a portly gentleman called, tromping into the room. "Irma and Lawrence just finished their smooching. Now we can get everything set up."

"Set up? What?"

Intrigued, Betty watched him carry a giant boom box to a claw-footed table in one corner. He plugged the tape player in, then inserted a cassette he took from a shoe box. When he punched a button, Big Band music filled the room.

"Benny Goodman!" he shouted, grinning as he snapped his fingers to the swing beat. He rolled up the rugs and pushed them against the far wall.

A lanky, handsome woman with blue-gray hair sailed into the room carrying a big grocery sack. "I've got the punch!" Lucille Clooney hefted milk jugs from her pa-

per sack. From them she poured a light-purple punch into the bowl. "Grape Surprise," Lucille told her, smiling. "I only make this about once a year, but I'm sure famous for it. I know you've heard about my good Grape Surprise punch already."

Betty hesitated, decided that a white lie was justified for making a nice old lady happy, and nodded. "People tell me there's nothing else like it."

Lucille chortled and tucked the empty milk jugs under the table. A few seconds later people began crowding into the room, led by Norma. Max brought up the rear, with two delicate, bent little ladies holding his arms.

Immediately he looked toward Betty. Streams of desire ran through her at the way his eyes sought her out and absorbed her greedily. As he escorted the ladies to chairs he patiently measured his long stride to their tiny ones, but after he helped them to their seats, he pivoted and strode through the crowd toward Betty's serving table.

She found herself clasping a long-handled spoon to keep her hands still. His black boots made heavy, commanding sounds on the wooden floor, and his big-shouldered body moved with mesmerizing grace under the dashing black suit. It dawned on her that he looked more like an elegant Old West gunfighter than a country judge.

He stopped directly across the table from her and finally pulled his gaze away long enough to glance at the line of serving pans. "You did it," he admitted. "I apologize for doubting you."

His admiration warmed her to a troublesome degree. She wanted him like the sun wants to shine, and she couldn't, wouldn't, let herself have him. But she could smile at him and revel in his compliment. "Have something to eat," she offered. "There are ribs, and chopped chicken for sandwiches, and Brunswick stew; coffee, iced tea—"

"I'll save mine for later."

"This sample would be on the house."

He shook his head slightly, green eyes amused as they held her attention. Behind the amusement was something darker, a reckless promise he wanted her to share, a wildness that could be hers if she would only agree.

Their strained, silent communication was broken by the sudden arrival of a dozen more people, who hadn't attended the wedding. Irma and Lawrence posed in a corner, having their pictures taken by a friend with a camera. They waved to the new people and called for them to come over.

Max turned slowly and stared at the newcomers in dismay. Betty hid her smile behind a hand. "Your plans went awry. We must have thirty people here. It's a good thing I always bring extra food."

She knelt and began checking covered pans filled with cole slaw and baked beans. "They're going to clean me out." Already people were lined up at the table's end, and the first had begun piling sliced pickles on his plastic plate.

Some of the elderly people were frail; none were wealthy, judging by their clean but worn-looking finery. But all seemed to be anticipating a wonderful evening, and their eyes gleamed as they looked at dinner.

Max grumbled under his breath but leaned over the table and whispered to her. "I want this bunch to have a great dinner and a great time." He sounded regretful, but determined. "So use all the food you brought. Don't put anything aside for our dinner. You've escaped a skirmish, at least for tonight. Relax and enjoy yourself."

Betty's mouth popped open in surprise. Disappointment cut into her teasing mood. It made her realize that she'd been looking forward to their dinner despite her resentment. "I . . . well . . . how do you like steaks?" she blurted.

He was clearly astonished. Then he arched a brow. "Cooked."

"Good choice. I have two or three T-bones in the bus's refrigerator."

"I have some gnarled baking potatoes that aren't too far gone."

"I'll provide the beef, and you provide the spuds. How about that?"

"Fantastic." He looked at her with so much pleasure that she sat back on her heels and smiled at him foolishly. Puzzlement crept into his expression. "Why the change of heart?"

She quickly brought her smile into a neutral range. With a shrug she said, "You're a nice man. I don't want you to miss dinner."

He was silent. Then, "You're a nice lady. I don't want you to be uncomfortable around me anymore. I really would like to be your friend."

He spoke without any hint of teasing. Betty was so touched that affection poured into her like water filling an empty vessel. *I've been looking for you all my life,* she told him silently.

She dropped her gaze to a pan of biscuits under the table and pretended to scrutinize them. "Then I'll be comfortable."

"Good."

People began coming down the line, serving themselves from the trays and pans. Already they were murmuring about the barbecue's delicious aroma, and when several taste-tested bits of it, they exclaimed with appreciation.

Betty stood. "I have to go to work now," she told Max softly, hating to end their conversation.

"You work. I'll watch."

He reached for a piece of barbecue, but a wizened, grinning lady interrupted him. She thumped one of his thick shoulders. "Care to dance, boy?" Someone had turned up the volume on the boom box. The matron winked at Betty. "Can I swipe him from you?"

"I give you permission," she said quaintly.

The woman peered at Max. "Can you shake a leg to this old music?"

Max drew himself up and looked at her with mock amazement. "I'm Bartram Templeton's son. I can dance your shoes off."

She giggled and wagged a bony finger at him. "You're just as smooth as your daddy was. But you behave, now. I'm too old to do anything but dance. Come on."

Max laughed and led her away. Betty turned toward the line of people and busied herself checking the food. *He's his father's son. Don't forget that,* she reminded herself.

The food was gobbled up within an hour, and only the birdlike appetites of some of the guests let Betty's supplies stretch to accommodate everyone. She had a ball talking to the people and listening to their excited compliments, but she was exhausted by the time they finished eating.

She hadn't worked hard enough to be so tired. No, she was drained from the tension that always simmered inside her when she was around Max. Before she began cleaning up, she took some time to feast on the sight of him dancing. He moved with a grace that belied his brawn; he laughed often, the sound distinct and luxurious above the music.

And after he removed his long coat, she glanced around the room and noticed that age made no difference when it came to ogling a handsome man. Many bifocals were adjusted so that Max's physique could be studied discreetly.

"Sugar, you look so pooped, you deserve a reward," the punch lady said.

Betty tore her gaze away from Max and smiled at Lucille, who held out a glass cup filled with Grape Surprise. "Why, thank you." She took the cup, hiding her reluctance. After having suffered through a pudgy adolescence that extended well into college, she'd vowed

to stay slender. These southern-style punch drinks were little more than sugar and water. She loved them.

Betty took a swallow. The mixture had a pleasant sharpness to it that was different from any punch she'd tasted before. She looked at Lucille curiously. "Lemon juice?"

Lucille hooted. "That's it. Lemon juice." She winked, then wandered away, her own cup of punch swaying in her hand.

Betty took another swallow. This stuff was great. Barely sweet. She could indulge without too much guilt. She tipped the cup back and downed the contents.

Suddenly she decided that she was too warm. Drinking more punch would cool her off. She sauntered over to the bowl, filled the cup again, and sat down in a chair by the punch table. She took several hearty swallows from her cup while she watched the dancers. She began to grin and tap one foot to the beat. Big Band music was *marvelous*. Lord, she'd never enjoyed herself so much. She decided to buy a whole collection of Benny Goodman music.

Rats. Her cup was empty again. The prissy things were so small. She reached over and dipped it into the punch bowl, then tilted her head back and gulped the punch in one long swallow. Immediately she refilled the cup.

Four cups of punch in five minutes. Lord, she was being a pig! Betty thumped the empty cup on the table and stared at Max, who was bebopping with a woman who could have doubled for Grandma Moses. Betty let her gaze wander over him. She sighed in appreciation.

Suddenly all the blood in her body rushed to one area, throbbing, aching inside her veins. Why was she resisting him? She couldn't remember. She wanted to ask Max to please, *please* dance with her. A slow dance. She wanted to rub against him and slide her hands down his long, tapering back to the tight mounds of his rump.

She chuckled hoarsely. She'd grab him! But then

she'd apologize by gently rubbing circles on those hard, flexing muscles, while she nuzzled his neck. It was so warm in this place!

She fanned herself and continued indulging her fantasy. She'd stroke her hands over those big, lean thighs, too, holding him close to her, so close. She shut her eyes and imagined exactly how hard he'd feel and how good. Wouldn't it be fun to turn this fantasy into reality? She'd get up right now and go to him. . . .

Betty jerked her eyes open in alarm. These thoughts were getting out of control. What was wrong with her? She had to start stacking her pans and trays. Yes. Whew! Her stomach felt a little strange.

No excuse, she told herself sternly. Work. Up and at 'em. Nobody was ever going to call her a pampered little fat girl again. Betty rubbed her forehead, confused. No one had called her that in years.

She planted her hands on the table and bounced to her feet. A strange thing happened. Her knees tried to kiss each other. Someone had stolen all of her bones.

Staring down into the bowl of purple punch, she dimly recalled feeling this way once or twice during college. At sorority parties. Betty gasped. "I'm *drunk*," she said aloud. The horror of her situation sobered her a little. Her heart beating wildly, she looked around to see if anyone had heard. But everyone was dancing. It hurt her eyes to watch them, so she quickly looked away, blinking rapidly.

Reputation. Ruined. Not cool. Walk outside and hide in bus. Make straight line to door. Move slowly. Move . . . feet. Smile. Don't stagger. Forget smile. Too much to coordinate.

She managed to leave the reception room without bumping into anything or anyone. In the foyer she went to the front door and squinted at the door knob, then put one hand on it experimentally. Damned complicated thing.

"Betty? You all right?"

Norma had come down the hall beside the wedding

parlor. Now she stopped. Betty swayed. "What's in that punch?"

Norma gasped softly. "Don't you know?"

"Uh oh. Bad news. Can you . . . can you turn this doorknob for me?"

"Wait here. I'll get Max."

"Okay."

Norma hurried away and Betty fumbled with the door knob until it turned. She found her way onto the veranda and down the steps to the lawn. The cool night air cleared her head a little. She wandered around the lawn, looking up at the night sky, enjoying the stars.

She heard heavy footsteps on the veranda. Then they softened. She turned toward them unsteadily. Max crossed the lawn to her and grasped her under the elbows. He was a large, dark, comforting shape. "Earth to celestial navigator," he said solemnly. "Are you off course?"

She clutched his shirtfront. Abruptly she felt foolish and afraid. But it was all right to tell Max. She could tell Max anything. "I'm so embarrassed."

"How many cups of punch did you have?"

Slowly she held up one hand. "Pick some fingers. Four, I think." She grabbed his shoulders and tried to shake him. "I didn't know, Maximilian! I didn't know. It all happened so quick. Zoom! Boom!"

"You drank four cups of punch one right after the other?"

"It was good punch!"

"Oh, babe," he said sympathetically, and drew her into a deep embrace. She burrowed her face against his chest and made snuffling sounds. He stroked her hair. "That punch is a local tradition. Everybody knows about it."

" 'Cept me."

"I thought someone had told you. It's made with moonshine. A *lot* of moonshine, carefully disguised."

"Agggh."

"Be happy. I think you've set a record. I can't recall anyone drinking that much that quick and still being able to walk. You're one tough lady."

As he finished, her knees buckled. "Bye-bye," she said solemnly as she began sliding down his torso.

Chuckling, he bent quickly and picked her up. "Relax. I'll take care of you."

"Okay." She patted his chest. "Good ol' marine." She tilted her head back, dug her fingers into his string tie, and gave it several jerks. "Don't let anybody see me like this. Don't. I'm so afraid. What would they think? My work. My reputation." She emphasized each word by tugging at his string tie.

He coughed and said in a strangled voice, "Let go of my tie. Put your hand in your lap. Yes, like that. Thank you."

"Hide me."

Max chuckled. "Mind if I carry you up to my house and have my way with you?"

She flopped an arm over his shoulders. "Go ahead. No problem." He was only teasing. But she could hope, couldn't she?

Six

Having a code of honor was hell. Max reflected on all the times in his life when he'd refused to take advantage of women who had imbibed a little too much for their dignity's good.

His motives hadn't been entirely selfless—when he took a woman to bed, he wanted her to remember him in glorious, crystal-clear detail the next morning. Rejecting what was recklessly offered hadn't always been easy, but he'd never regretted doing so, and he'd earned a lot of morning-after gratitude from embarrassed women with hangovers.

None of those women, however, had been Betty Quint. Right now, with Betty's taut, round hips snuggled against his outer thigh and her back curled against his side, he wondered if his honor could stand the challenge. Max rubbed his cheek on her rose-scented hair and shifted his arm on the back of the couch to curve the hollow of his shoulder closer to her.

His arousal became a torment. He propped his sock-clad feet on a black coffee table of oriental design and stretched a little, wishing that he had traded his black marrying suit for the accommodating comfort of sweatpants and a long-tailed football jersey.

Obviously unaware of the sublime pain she was caus-

ing, Betty munched potato chips loudly, then sighed, "Hmmmm."

The sensual sound made Max shut his eyes in dismay. He nuzzled her hair. "You're enjoying your dinner, I take it?"

She wiggled her bare feet against a pillow on the sleek black couch and hiccuped softly. "Love the food. Love this place. What a surprise you are, Maximilian. You've turned this sweet old country house into a lovely samurai warrior's den." She leaned her head back on his shoulder and chuckled. "You need a geisha."

"Oh, I'd rather have you, instead. A female samurai."

She growled fiercely. "I'm tough. Gimme a sharp charge card, and I'll leave a trail of destruction through Neiman-Marcus that you wouldn't believe."

"I can't picture you as the type who cut her teeth on a silver spoon. That kind of woman usually wants to be pampered. You seem to thrive on hard work."

She crunched another potato ship and nodded fervently. "When I turned eighteen, my parents kicked me out of the nest and told me to fly or fall."

Max craned his head and studied her in amazement. "Why?"

"Because they didn't want me to turn out like a lot of my friends—lazy, snotty little debutantes with no idea what the real world was like." She hiccuped again. "I admit, I was headed in that direction."

"Don't feel bad. When I was a teenager, I stole cars."

"How exciting! Did you ever get caught?"

"No. Norma's son and I used to swipe whatever we could hot-wire, take it for a joy ride, then abandon it on a deserted back road. We were damned good at our little hobby, but we were headed for trouble. I think a lot of people were betting that we'd end up in jail someday. They were relieved when we joined the marines."

She clucked in exaggerated rebuke. "You sound proud. But would you want *your* children to steal cars?"

Max grinned. "Only if they were as good at it as I was."

"Bad! You're so bad, Maximilian." She sighed pensively. "You have so much fun. I'm so boring and normal."

"Thank you for classifying me as abnormal," he protested solemnly.

She laughed, the sound lovely and warm, then missed her mouth with a potato chip. The chip crumbled on her chin and flakes scattered over her sweater. Max fought a strong urge to pick up the flakes that landed on her breasts.

"What a slob," she said cheerfully, and popped each broken bit into her mouth.

Max adored her comfortable earthiness. "No manners. I like that in a person."

"What? No manners? I was schooled in etiquette by Miss Louise Vanagrette of the Greenbriar Cotillion. I have manners out the wazoo, Maximilian."

She tilted her head so that she could peer up at him. Max looked at her half-shut eyes and flushed cheeks. In the cozy light of a floor lamp her full, wide mouth beckoned him with a crooked smile that was both comical and provocative. If he kissed her right now, she'd probably laugh—but she'd kiss him back.

While he considered the possibilities, he stroked a crumb of potato chip from her lower lip. "I'm glad you're here. My house feels like it has life in it now."

"It's a fabulous old house, Maximilian. Your father left it to you?"

"Yes. Along with a lot of furniture that's been in the family for decades. Most of it's stored up in the attic. You'd probably love it, but my taste runs to this."

He gestured around them at walls hung with bright Japanese wood-block prints. Most showed battles and warriors, but a few depicted wildly costumed Kabuki actors and sprawling Oriental landscapes. His furniture was sparse and simple, all sleek blacks and whites. "I collected this furniture and artwork over the years," he told her. "But I kept most of it in storage until I had a permanent home for it." He pointed toward a large,

muted tapestry on the wall across from the couch. "I like the lines of those abstract patterns. They're both peaceful and aggressive. How you interpret them depends on your point of view."

"I feel peaceful." She drew a single chip from the bowl on her lap, brought it to her mouth with the slow grace of an unsteady hand, then laid the chip on her tongue. It disappeared between her lips without a sound.

"Very nice," Max whispered, mesmerized. "I'm thrilled that you like my interior decorating." He spoke to her in a low, seductive tone guaranteed to keep the kiss-me expression on her face.

She blinked swiftly, as if realizing that she was tip-toeing into dangerous territory. "Oh, I'm bad. I'm so bad. I feel so tempted. I could just go wild."

"Sssh, Betty, nothing is going to happen until you're—"

"Take these away." She handed the bowl of potato chips to him. "Or I'll keep eating until they're all gone."

Max felt disgusted, but had to strangle a laugh. At least she wasn't worrying about other temptations. Good. Temptation could sneak up on her that way. "Betty, Betty," he chided softly, setting the bowl of chips aside. "Why are you so afraid of indulging yourself?"

She hiccuped, then turned her face toward him and rested her forehead against his jaw. "You don't understand," she murmured. "You don't have a monogram like mine."

"A monogram?"

She let her hands settle loosely on her lap. He doubted that she was aware that the fingers of one hand trailed over onto his thigh. He decided to enjoy the torturous little pleasure in noble silence. "My monogram," she repeated. She sighed. "My parents have terrible notions of what's funny. My middle name is . . . is *Belle*."

"So? Betty Belle . . . Quint." He groaned, then began to smile. "So your initials are B-B-Q."

"Stop that. Stop it. I can feel you smiling. My forehead can feel your jaw muscles moving. Stop it."

He raised a hand to the black luxury of her hair and playfully tugged at one of the combs that swept it back from her face. He slipped the comb free. "Relax, Betty Belle." Max tossed the comb somewhere on the smoky gray carpet behind the couch. He ran his splayed fingers across her temple and into the loosened strands. "Relax. Keep talking."

"Mmmm. Mmmm. Max. No. Oh, Max. Oh, hell." She turned a little more toward him, and her willful hand moved an inch across his thigh. "Nice."

"Talk," he ordered. His voice was strained with desire. He stared at her hand.

"Ol' B-B-Q. That's me. It's funny now, but when I was a child, it was a horrible name. I was, shall we say, a bit short for my weight." She cleared her throat and amended drolly, "Oh, let's be honest. I was a baby whale. Whenever my parents took me on vacation to the ocean, I felt an urge to migrate and search for my herd."

Max bit his lip and struggled not to laugh out loud. "Babe, if it's any consolation, you look fantastic now. All that blubber has become one helluva pretty body."

She patted his thigh heartily. "And I have great fins."

Max sucked a deep breath. His voice came out a dry rasp. "I hope you remember how to surface for air. It might come in handy when we really get into deep water."

Her hand lay still again. "So, anyway, I was fat." Her voice was a little bitter and sad. "And my initials were B-B-Q. I suffered through an awful list of nicknames. Spare Ribs. Pork Belly. Betty Burp. Anytime another kid got mad at me, I heard those names."

He winced a little and stroked her hair in sympathy. "If we were both ten years old, I'd go out on the playground tomorrow and blacken some eyes on your behalf."

Her soft giggles were disarmingly pleasant. "Where were you when I needed you?"

"Waiting. Just waiting to meet you."

They were both silent for a minute. She curled and uncurled her hand atop his thigh, not really squeezing the muscle there, but creating languid waves of sensation nonetheless.

"Max, I didn't lose weight until I was in college. I started exercising and eating right, and I haven't had a problem since. But I've had a lot of trouble learning to love myself." She hesitated, then added softly, "I think that's why I was so vulnerable when I met my musician, Sloan Richards. I still felt like a homely dumpling, and he taught me to feel pretty. He was every daydream I'd ever had come true."

Max didn't like the wistfulness in her voice when she discussed the musician. Sloan Richards. He filed the name away for future inspection. "Look at me," he commanded.

"Bossy." She raised her head, frowning.

Max caught her chin in his hand and held her still as he searched her heavy-lidded eyes. "Forget the musician. You learned what you needed to learn from him, and that's all he was good for. You're beautiful. Believe it."

Her expression softened. "I've already forgotten him." Her voice was breathless. "Now I'd like to know what I can learn from you."

She shoved past his restraining hand and kissed him. Her tongue slid inside his mouth like a slow, lazy river, filling him with her erotic energy. Honor was temporarily forgotten as he pulled her to him and clasped the back of her head, urging her to continue.

They both shivered, and as she angled her mouth in new directions she inhaled with quick, ragged puffs. Max felt adamant needs rise inside him, but he forced himself to keep control.

This woman was heaven and hell, like no other. Her kisses were bawdy, but from the back of her throat came sweet, almost keening, sounds. Her hand trembled on his thigh, but then moved upward, stroking him through his trousers and feathering excitedly over

the part of him that immediately strained toward her caress.

Honor. It taunted him. Her mouth held the poignantly sweet taste of grape juice, and he thought of the damned Grape Surprise, with its enormous volume of moonshine. *She's drunk*, he reminded himself fiercely. *You can't let her do something she really will regret.*

Oh, but for a minute longer he did, until he had to push himself away from her eager mouth and take her hand in his for self-protection. "We don't want to do this tonight," he told her, but silently cursed the lack of conviction in his voice.

Disappointment filled her eyes. "Parts of us certainly do."

"Those parts don't have brains. What happened to your determination to stay away from me?"

Her face flamed with embarrassment, and she frowned sadly, looking confused. "I know; I'm being irresponsible."

He shook her gently. "You're not irresponsible. You're human. I don't want you to avoid me, but I don't want to wake up in the morning and have you tell me that what we've done is a mistake."

"I . . . I *know* that you're not right for me." She shut her eyes, making an obvious and painful-looking effort to think clearly. When she looked at him again, tears shimmered on her lower lashes. "But you're so wonderful. Why do you have to be so wonderful, you jackass?"

Her combination of regret and devotion nearly tore him apart. "I just can't help myself," he said grimly. He blew a long breath, trying to exhale his own confusion and self-rebuke.

It would be simple to sweep away the only obstacle that was keeping them apart. All he had to do was change his mind about marriage; all he had to do was tell her that someday, yes, he could imagine signing a formal document that pledged his life to another person. He wouldn't even have to tell her that he wanted to pledge his life to *her* specifically. She'd be satisfied with just knowing that he wasn't against marriage in general.

He started to say that he'd reconsidered, but his conscience burned the words before they could leave his throat. It was a lie. If he said that he'd changed his mind, he'd be lying to himself as well as to her. And she deserved better than that. He wanted her to have the best, or at least what her convictions told her was the best. He wanted her to be happy. He'd never wanted so badly to protect someone else's ideals at the expense of his own needs.

Max twisted away from her, pulled his feet from the coffee table, and smiled sarcastically. Very damned noble, he told himself. Now suffer. He raked his hands through his hair and stared at the floor. Slowly she rearranged herself, holding the couch's overstuffed upholstery for support, until she was seated as he was, facing forward, both feet firmly on the floor.

"I feel like a tease," she whispered miserably. "It's a first."

"You were ready to go for broke, babe. That wasn't teasing."

"Then why do you have an evil, Jack Nicholson-playing-the-devil smile on your face?"

"Because I'm contemplating my life."

"Don't. It looks painful."

"I should never have left the marines. The choices were simpler there."

"What choices?"

"Exactly."

He stood up, frustrated by a self-examination that led back to the same answer as always. He had lost the ability to take leaps of faith. Oh, he was flexible in the small ways, the everyday things, but he couldn't buck the big issues. For two decades he'd had a front-row view of the world's insanity, and he'd lost his vision of paradise forever. Happiness for him would have to be based on what he could see and hold and measure each day without questioning whether it would exist the day after.

Max pivoted toward her angrily. " 'Come into my guest

room, said the spider to the fly.' " He tried to ignore her sorrowful, yearning gaze. "In the morning you can load your hangover onto the barbecue bus and drive home. Will the mutant cat survive the night without you?"

After a second her expression became resigned. "Yes. She has lots of food and water, and a fresh kitty litter box."

"Ah. What more could a creature want?" He smiled tightly, thinking of too many answers to that question as he looked down at her.

She staggered to her feet and listed sideways. Max caught her arm and drew her close. She raised her big silver eyes and nearly dissolved his restraint with a look of poignant affection. "I like chicken salad. Do you like chicken salad?"

"No. I ate canned chicken salad once in 'Nam and almost died from food poisoning."

"Oh."

"Are you trying to tell me that you're still hungry? You ate two peanut butter-and-jelly sandwiches and half a bag of potato chips."

She blinked owlishly. "I like to read those big family-saga books where everybody plots against everybody else."

"That's nice," he crooned. There was no point in aiming for logic in this conversation. She was endearing and sincere, but fading fast. "Come on and get in bed, and I'll tell you a good-night story."

"I'm just trying to find out what we have in common. What do you like to read?"

"Guerrilla Warfare Weekly," he joked.

She sputtered with laughter. "You like gorillas? We should visit Zoo Atlanta."

"I read magazines and newspapers. Current affairs."

Her eyes showed desperation. "How about this current affair?" She launched herself at him, throwing her arms around his neck and kissing him wildly.

Max stepped back with a barely concealed groan.

"Dammit, we've already discussed this. You're pie-eyed, so I forgive you. *But don't push me too far.*"

"Maybe I don't want to listen to my common sense anymore." She clasped his shirtfront. "Maybe I'm so lonely that I can barely stand my own company. Maybe I think that I'll go crazy if I don't get you out of my system. *You have to do something, Maximilian.*"

The short fuse on his control burst into flame. "You asked for it," he said angrily. He picked her up so swiftly that she yelped. Holding her tightly against his chest, he carried her through the living room and down a short hall, where he kicked open the door to the guest room.

"Max, Max, I'll take a chance on being sorry in the morning," she whispered raggedly as he crossed a room that still contained the pleasant, unassuming old furniture his father had left there. "I need you tonight."

Cursing under his breath, a little hurt, he laid her on a double bed, then jerked the quilt and sheet from under her. The bed's wooden frame creaked in rhythm with his movements. The darkness was thick, but when his fingers found the fastenings on her slacks, he moved with nimble speed. Within a few seconds he dragged the slacks over her legs and feet.

He threw the garment on the floor behind him and again found her with his hands. She gasped, not in surprise but in pleasure. Touching her made his head swim with desire; he gritted his teeth and stroked her through her panties, kneeling over her on the bed as he did.

The moans that cascaded from her throat were even more erotic because he couldn't see her. He could only feel her, her body incredibly aroused as he slid his fingers under the panties and between her legs. She reached for him, frantically stroking his knees and the arm he braced beside her.

"Max, I want to kiss you," she cried. "Don't stay there. Please, don't stay so far away. Lay down beside me."

He shivered in agony and lay down, sighing as he

received the wild hunger of her mouth. Her body arched and trembled; he heard himself making hoarse sounds in the back of his throat because his intimate touching revealed the delicacy and strength of her passion, passion that he wouldn't permit himself to sample in the way his body screamed for.

"Need you, want you," she called out, and then she seemed to focus all her power as she burst into soft mewling sounds and went very still, shuddering. He felt her sweet delirium with his hand, and wretchedly bent his head to her shoulder.

She quieted, relaxing. Her hands rose in the darkness and cupped his head, stroking his hair and face while she made gentle, tired noises. "Max, oh, Max," were the only coherent words she managed, and they were so filled with adoration that a knot rose in his throat.

"You're sleepy," he whispered, as if trying to hypnotize her.

"Max." Her hands moved lovingly, stroking the heart out of him, making him want to forget honor and take her as quickly as he could undress himself.

He thought of her reaction in the morning, when all she would remember was a drunken coupling with a man she had tried very hard to avoid. Max pushed himself away and stood beside the bed, then grabbed blindly for the covers and pulled them over her. This way, at least, he would leave their friendship unharmed, with the possibility of real passion someday, shared not from groggy desperation but from a sober change of heart—hers.

"Max . . . why?" she asked sadly, but her voice was sluggish with fatigue.

He leaned over her and brushed tangled hair from her forehead, crooning husky sounds to her while she sighed with pleasure at his slow caress. "Good night, babe," he whispered gruffly.

"Why?" she insisted, but even that brief word trailed off before she finished it.

He listened to her deep, even breathing. Then he placed a very light kiss on her mouth, whispering as he did, "Because, unfortunately for both of us, I love you."

She knew that if she opened her eyes, reality would sneak into her brain and confirm what she remembered from the night before. Betty fought for a moment, then took a deep breath and banished sleep.

Her head throbbed. She lifted it from the pillow and squinted at a lovely old room filled with Victorian wicker. Thin white drapes on an eastern window let a narrow band of sunshine peek under their hem. Her gaze found her black slacks folded neatly across a chair. Her black leather flats sat beside it. From the way they gleamed, Max might have polished them.

Swallowing hard, she eased her head back on the pillow and covered her face with both hands. Max was the most incredible man in the world.

She dressed and ran her hands through her hair. Her combs were laid out on a claw-footed nightstand beside the bed. There was also a masculine-looking hairbrush, which must have been Max's, a glass of water, and a bottle of aspirin. Written on a sheet of notebook paper in dark, verticle script was a message. *Good morning. The bathroom is down the hall on the right.*

She dressed, made an attempt to neaten her hair, and swallowed two aspirin. When she stepped into the hallway, she halted, cocking her head toward the end that went to the living room and kitchen. She heard a pan rattle and smelled the aroma of food.

Betty hurried to the bathroom, shut the door, and leaned against it, trembling. When she finally looked at herself in the large square mirror over a pedestal sink, she saw the self-rebuke and anguish in her eyes.

She washed her face briskly while she talked to herself in a stern whisper. By the time she walked to the kitchen, she felt stronger, if not better.

Max stood with his back to the door. His kitchen was a neat, regimented place without frills, but appealing. The old white appliances and aged tile floor had a scrubbed look; a dining island in the center of the room was set with blue stoneware plates and white napkins.

Watching Max at the stove, Betty grasped the door-jamb. Her knees felt weak. He looked so strong, so sure of himself. From the straight, broad back to the tightly molded hips and long, solid legs, he was a man of physical as well as spiritual power. He was dressed in brown corduroy trousers and a white dress shirt. His rich brown hair reflected golden highlights in the sunshine from a window over the sink.

She gathered her resolve and tried to speak normally. "Good morning."

He turned swiftly and looked at her. His expression was troubled but then lightened, though the change seemed to require effort. "Sleep well?"

"Yes, thank you." The polite exchange had very little to do with the real dialogue. Questions hung in the air between them. The kitchen seemed unnaturally quiet and still, as if its energy had been absorbed by the tension.

Tears burned the back of her throat, and suddenly she knew that she couldn't keep up the casual charade. She crossed the room swiftly, almost running, and grasped his hands.

Trembling and miserable, she looked up at him. "I used you and hurt you, and I'm so sorry."

"If it feels this good getting used and hurt—"

"What you did was the most unselfish—"

"Believe me, if you could have read my self-serving thoughts—"

"I won't ever throw myself at you again. I swear it."

The conversation crashed to a dead stop. Surprise and dismay darkened his eyes. His brawny hands tightened carefully on hers. "If you're trying not to hurt me, you just failed miserably."

"Nothing has changed." she told him wearily. "Except that now I know that I have less control over the situation than I thought."

"But now you should also know that you can relax. That I won't do anything to damage your feelings for me."

"The last thing I want to do is hurt you. Or myself."

"Good. Then we can—"

"I want you to do something for me that will be even more unselfish than what you did last night. I want you to do it because there's no other way we can keep from teasing each other." Tears sliding down her cheeks, she searched his eyes for a reaction.

"I'm listening," he said warily.

"Find someone else. As soon as you can."

Slowly he lifted her hands to the center of his chest. He held them there in a grip that was now more angry than caring. Against her palms she felt the fast, harsh beating of his heart. "You couldn't hurt me any worse if you tried," he said in a low, fierce tone.

"Do you think it was easy for me to say?" She shook her head wretchedly. "No."

"Any suggestions as to who your replacement should be?" His voice was acid. "Can you recommend someone in town? Or do you just assume that I'm so undiscriminating that any reasonably attractive, reasonably intelligent woman will do?"

She pulled her hands away, then roughly wiped her face. "You need a woman who doesn't want what I want."

His arms dropped to his sides. He studied her coldly. "If you're willing to give up what we have—what we *could* have—just because I won't offer you the false security of a wedding license, then we don't have as much going for us as I thought."

"It's not false security," she whispered. "Not when two people believe in it."

"I believe in you and me, together, each day, each night, making each other happy, sharing everything we have to share."

"Except the future."

"The future has no guarantees. Not just for marriage, but for anything. I've seen people shot, stabbed, blown up. They thought they had futures. They lived for their futures. They were wrong."

Energy left her. Tired, despondent, she stared at him dully. "No more games, Max. Let's stop pretending that either of us will compromise. Find someone else. I'm not going to let myself be alone with you again. It's finished."

"No, but the rules will be tougher from now on. Last night was your only reprieve. Next time don't expect self-sacrifice on my part."

"There won't be a next time." Even as she spoke she felt a jolt of fear—fear because deep down she already knew that they wouldn't be finished until one of them lost everything.

Seven

The black limousine purred up the hill as Max was lowering his flag for the day. He halted, amazed. In Webster Springs limousines were about as common as dinosaurs. A limosaur, that's what this was, he thought drolly. While it climbed toward his home, he felt a premonition of trouble, which he quickly attributed to his bad mood. But for an instant when the car paused at the top of the driveway, it caught the rays of the setting sun, its black sides flashing blood red, and Max, frowning, walked forward.

The car stopped at the edge of his lawn. A chauffeur got out, nodding a silent hello. The passenger opened a rear door before the chauffeur reached it, and Max knew the visitor's identity the moment he glimpsed a lion's mane of white hair.

T. S. Audubon. He had probably planned his arrival to coincide with the sunset's drama. Audubon loved to make an entrance.

He unfolded his tall, elegantly lean body from the limousine's seat and flashed a pleasant smile at Max. "Major, how nice to find you at home," he said in his aristocratic, tidewater Virginia accent as he extended a hand.

Max grasped it heartily, and respect flowed between

them as they traded shrewd assessments. "No style, as usual," he told Audubon, indicating Audubon's flaw-less black suit, which was double-breasted, very taste-ful, and undoubtedly very expensive.

Audubon laughed. "Are you wearing the flag these days? I admire your patriotism, but it clashes with your sweat suit."

Smiling ruefully, Max removed the flag from his shoul-der. "It's not my new uniform. I'm a civilian now, body and soul. Retired from the glory."

"Ah, Major. You may have left the marines, but you'll never retire. You and I are alike—we've spent too many years battling the shadows, and now we have trouble appreciating the light." Audubon shrugged gracefully. "We're too old to change our ways."

Max arched a brow. Audubon wasn't much older than he, despite the white hair. They had met in Viet-nam, though Audubon had been in the army, not the marines. Audubon had actually dropped out of college to enlist; he was one of the idealistic types, a poet and philosopher. But he had also been a fighter, and a top-notch sergeant. Behind his back his men had called him Ashley Wilkes, but with affection.

Audubon had never lost his idealism, his toughness, or his taste for adventure. His path had crossed Max's many times over the years.

"Let me guess," Max said casually. "You were just in the neighborhood and you decided to drop by for a cup of tea."

"Precisely. But I really can't stay long. I'm due back in Virginia before midnight."

"Business or pleasure?"

"Who can tell the difference anymore? But she's beau-tiful, so perhaps—"

Max laughed. "I wouldn't want you to miss a hot date, old boy. Come and have a spot of tea."

Audubon didn't discuss the real intent of his visit until he was standing in front of the fireplace in Max's

living room with a glass of cognac in one hand. Max lounged on the couch with his own glass.

"Here's to retirement," he told Audubon, raising his glass slightly, then taking a swallow.

Audubon merely smiled. He leaned against the mantel and crossed one handsomely shod foot over the other. Under thick white brows his eyes were patient. "You know this life isn't for you," he said finally.

"You're wrong."

"I have splendid opportunities for you. The work would suit you perfectly. Think of it, Major: the exotic locales, the exotic women, the intrigue, the excitement—"

"The jungles, the guns, the possibility that I might leave little pieces of my hide scattered all over some godforsaken place."

"Haven't you heard? I've expanded my services. I not only retrieve people, I protect people from needing retrieval. Douglas Kincaid, for example. He's both a good friend and a client of mine. He had a little problem with a project in Scotland a few months ago, and I brought a team of my people to his aid."

Max chuckled dryly. "No, Audubon, I can't see myself playing bodyguard for the rich and famous. Besides, I suspect that those assignments are *not* commonplace."

"Well, if you've become *soft*, I'm sure I could find unchallenging, safe, sweet little tasks for you to perform."

Laughing, Max toasted him. "You manipulative SOB. Don't try to embarrass me into working for you. I've spent the past twenty years doing my part to make the world a safer place to live. I have the medals and the scars to prove it."

Audubon's expression darkened. "You gave up the ability to be a passive spectator. You won't ever get it back. Stop trying."

"Speaking of scars, how is Kyle Surprise doing?"

Exasperation mingled with the grimace on Audubon's patrician face. "He's happily married. And retired. Dammit."

Max gloated cheerfully. "Good to hear it. And his brother?"

"Jeopard's married too. And about to become a father. And retired. Dammit."

Max sat forward and struggled not to laugh again. Audubon wasn't accustomed to losing his best agents, and the fact that they'd left his employ for reasons as mundane as marriage obviously grated on him. He and Max shared the same opinion of marriage.

Max thought of Betty, and his humor faded. He'd certainly make her happy if he left town to work for Audubon. One of them deserved to be happy here, and it might as well be she.

"Oh, no," Audubon said grimly.

"What?"

"The look on your face. I mentioned Kyle's and Jeopard's marriages and your eyes immediately glazed over with pathetic sentiment. Don't tell me. You *wouldn't*."

"Get married? No." Max downed the rest of his drink in one gulp. "Not me. Never."

"Who is she? Just for the record."

"Mind your own business, old boy. She's no threat. I've already told her the hard, cold facts. She's already told me what I could do with my facts. So relax."

Audubon set his glass on the mantel. Smiling slyly, he slipped a hand inside his coat, then walked over to the coffee table and laid a business card down. It was the shade of champagne. Embossed on it was only a telephone number. "Work where you can do the most good," he cajoled in a smooth, confident tone. "I hate to be crass, but I must also mention that there would be a great deal of money involved."

"I have a good pension. I have money in savings. I have a tidy little salary as a magistrate—"

"But, surely, if you hope to win your lady's favor— without marrying her, of course—you could use more money."

Max frowned, thinking of Betty's privileged background. He'd never considered it an obstacle before,

but maybe it was. She obviously had a great deal of money. After all, how many people could pour thousands of dollars into a new business and buy a home plus fifty acres at the same time?

"I see the speculation on your face. Think about my offer," Audubon told him. "I'll always have room among my people for a man of your caliber. You could have your choice of interesting, not to mention honorable, assignments. You really could make the world a better place, Major."

Slowly Max picked up the card. "Or never see the good that already exists."

"There's much more evil than good. Trust me. Good night, Max."

Max walked with him to the porch. Audubon went to his limousine and left in the same stately manner in which he'd arrived. Max leaned against a porch post and gazed blindly into the night, thinking of Betty, thinking of the goodness that lay just beyond his reach.

She knew Max would show up. And he did. Midway through the afternoon on the restaurant's opening day, he sauntered into the main room. Earlier in the day he'd sent a large flower arrangement.

Betty forced herself to concentrate on the family of tourists, all five of whom wore T-shirts proclaiming, "I fell for the fall leaves in Webster Springs." She *had* to stay focused. The room was almost half full, an unexpected crowd for what should have been the mid-afternoon doldrums.

But she hadn't seen Max in two weeks. She was desperate for a supply of Max-appeal. And she was terrified that he'd realize that fact the minute he got close to her. *There won't be any reprieve for you next time,* he'd warned.

He spoke to the hostess, a sweet-faced little woman who also doubled as cashier at the stand in the hallway. She nodded and grinned, then led him to a table

near the tourist family's. "He asked for a table in your section," she told Betty merrily.

Betty nodded and politely finished with the family's order, while she tapped a nervous rhythm with the toe of her tennis shoe. She wiped sweaty palms on her blue jumper, then forced herself to stroll over to Max with a look of benign welcome.

He leaned back in his chair and continued to smile at her, not speaking. She was so full of conflicting emotions that they crowded her throat and she couldn't speak either, so she stopped at his table and simply looked at him.

His teasing smile faded. He sat forward slowly, his eyes never leaving hers. The pure man-woman communication he sent her way was staggering. They had a hungry gleam, but not for barbecue. She had been miserable during the past two weeks, and now she was floating in a dazed dimension where time stood still.

This was terrible, terrible. She shook her head. "Hi."

He propped his chin on one hand. "Hi."

"Nice to see you."

"Nice to see you."

"I had a great lunch crowd. I couldn't believe it on opening day. Andy didn't expect it either. We're short staffed. So I'm waiting on tables."

"I see."

Silence reigned again. She wanted to drop down in the chair beside his and lean close enough to count the blue flecks that hid among the green in his eyes. A perfectly reasonable need. Certainly.

"Thank you for the flowers."

"You're welcome. I like your hair in a ponytail. And I like your earrings. Silver looks good on you."

"They belonged to my grandmother Quint."

"She might have bought them from my grandfather. For a long time he ran the only general store in Webster Springs. Died when I was about twelve. He was a retired sailor. Had a peg leg."

"You're kidding."

"No. His nickname was Stumpy."

"Stumpy Templeton," she echoed solemnly. "He probably bought moonshine from *my* grandfather. Queasy Quint."

Max's mouth twitched with humor. "Probably. I never knew your grandfather."

"Me neither. He died before I was born."

"Like I told you once, my grandpa made great barbecue. It's been, oh, more than twenty-five years since I had any, but the memory is indelibly printed on my tongue."

"I'll have to fix your tongue."

"Oh? In public? Will you respect me later?"

She backed up a step and lifted her notepad, then drawled, "Take a look at the menu, mister. I ain't got all day. You need a written invitation or are you just here to gawk?"

"Gawking is my specialty. But I'll have some kind of chicken plate. Surprise me. And coffee."

"Coming right up."

"Hey, waitress," he said softly as she turned away. "Give me special attention. I'll leave you a big tip."

"Good. I could use the money."

"I could use the attention."

"Couldn't we all?"

"Betty hurried to the kitchen, her nerves in shambles, her body jumbled inside. He wasn't kidding, but then neither was she.

The Fates had obviously declared that today would be unusual. While she was in the kitchen dodging Andy and the other waitresses, the hostess came back and handed her a business card. "I just seated Frank Werner from Goody Foods. He wants to know if you have time to talk."

Betty grimaced at the card. "Tell Mr. Werner that his lunch is on the house. But I won't be able to talk to him until I get my customers served."

"Okay."

Andy was watching her with anxious eyes. "Isn't Goody Foods a big company? I mean, a national company?"

"Yes, one of the biggest."

"You wouldn't sell your sauce recipe to a bunch of stuffed shirts, would you? It'll always be your secret, won't it?"

She laughed. Even Andy didn't know how the sauce was made. She fixed it by herself in huge quantities that she stored in five-gallon jars. "Andy, this barbecue sauce is a Quint family inheritance. It will *never* belong to anyone else."

He stirred a pan of cole slaw with renewed vigor and looked relieved.

Out in the dining room Max just looked. He looked her over from head to toe as she carried a big mug of coffee to him. She spotted Frank and waved at him. He waved back. Max looked at Frank. Max then looked at her with one brow arched in dismay.

The combination of his presence plus the fatigue of opening-day jitters and Frank's arrival made her feel giddy. As she set the coffee in front of Max, she bent and whispered, "He's after my sauce."

Max's slit-eyed attention glided to Frank Werner again, then back to her. "I hope you mean that in a culinary way."

"He's vice president in charge of new products at Goody Foods' corporate headquarters in Atlanta. He's been after me for years to sell my recipe. About every six months he calls or sends a note. Now he can track me down in public."

"I could fix it so that he never wants to come back to Webster Springs again."

"How?"

Max smiled mysteriously. "Oh, he might get some speeding tickets. Or his car could be impounded for violating some obscure code." He sighed. "But, of course, I'm just the local magistrate. I have no control over how my old fishing buddy, the sheriff, treats a suspicious out-of-towner."

She wanted to kiss him. "Maximilian, many people have told me what a scrupulously fair judge you are. But thank you for offering to be crooked for my benefit."

"Oh, so you've been asking around about me again, have you?"

"Drink your coffee," she said immediately. "And be sure to burn your tongue." A minute later she brought him a plate filled with chicken, slaw, pickles, and a bowl of Brunswick stew, plus a basket of biscuits. "This is on the house, you lovely troublemaker. Prepare for ecstasy."

He shot her a somewhat rebuking look. "I keep waiting. Someday. Soon. If you come to your senses."

"I'm off to chat with the Goody man."

"I reserve my next comment on the grounds that you'd probably hit me for it."

Laughing, she went over and sat with Frank. He petted her ego, praised the restaurant decor, and exclaimed over his lunch, while she nodded politely and tried to keep from turning around to see how Max was faring with his lunch. She needed Max's praise. She felt like a schoolgirl waiting for her first kiss.

Frank finished by pulling a sheaf of papers from his coat pocket. He presented them to her and watched hopefully as she scanned the figures. "What do you think?"

"This is better than ever, Frank. I could be rich."

"Just say the word, Betty."

She put the papers down. "But if I do things my own way, I could be richer."

His happy expression fell. "I guess I'll check back with you in another six months."

"Anytime, Frank. You're always welcome to a free meal at my restaurant."

"Give me a hint, Betty. Just tell me *one* of the ingredients in your sauce that makes it unique."

"Honey from love-starved bees."

"Really?"

"No."

He groaned.

She reached across the checkered tablecloth and patted his arm. "Sorry." *Speaking of love starved . . .* She glanced toward Max.

His table and his plate were empty.

"Excuse me, Frank," she said quickly, and went to the cashier's stand. "Did Max Templeton leave?"

"Hmmm. A minute ago."

"Did he say anything?"

"No. He looked kind of puzzled. Like he was thinking about a problem and couldn't quite figure it out."

"He didn't say whether or not his food was good?"

"No, but he took all of his chicken with him. He had it wrapped up in a napkin. Ugh. It was messy too. Hey, he left you a five-dollar tip! And this."

She handed Betty a napkin that had been folded several times. "For Betty. Confidential" was written on the outside. She opened it so fast that she almost tore the paper. And when she read the note, with its coy little mushroom drawing underneath, her knees went weak.

She had won the skirmishes, but with this weapon he might very well win the war.

Max swiped his hand across the top of another cardboard box, then twisted away as a cloud of fine dust rose in the air. It floated in the harsh light of a bare bulb that hung from the attic's rafters. Max noticed that night had fallen outside a tiny octagonal window. Surprised, he glanced at his watch and discovered that he'd been in the attic for almost six hours.

Boxes that had once been stacked neatly against a wall now circled him, crammed haphazardly on the cloth-draped furniture that was stored in the attic. With their flaps open the boxes made Max think of ugly, square flowers in full bloom.

Flowers that hadn't yet produced the seed he wanted.

Scowling, he faced forward on the rump-sprung old

couch and tore yellowed sealing tape from the box between his feet. This box looked as if it hadn't been opened for decades. He pulled the flaps up and looked inside.

"Eureka!"

The box was full of books, and the one on top had a torn gray dust jacket with "Best-Loved Recipes" stamped in faded black ink. Max thumbed through the book quickly, studying notes scrawled in pencil, carefully unfolding recipes cut from newspapers and stored within the pages of the book.

The handwriting was his grandfather's, he suspected. Grandmother Templeton had died long before Max was born; besides, his grandfather had loved to cook, and Max recalled that his expertise in the kitchen—especially with barbecue sauce—had been the subject of much respectful teasing in the family.

The box was full of cookbooks. Max eagerly went through them page by page. He found several recipes for barbecue sauce, but all were simple and ordinary. None mentioned mushrooms.

He was so engrossed that the sound of a car cresting the ridge failed to register. Finally he realized that he had a visitor. Frowning, he dusted off his jeans and sweatshirt and hurried down the flight of narrow stairs behind the kitchen.

Betty was waiting for him on the front porch, her chin up, her eyes cold. She still wore the tennis shoes, blue jumper, and white top that he'd admired at the restaurant that afternoon. She hadn't come directly from work, though, because sprawled at the end of a rhinestone-dotted leash was Faux Paw.

"Why, it's Sheena of the Jungle," Max said dryly.

His teasing words failed to break the tension.

Betty gave him a withering stare. "I told you that I'd never let myself be alone with you again. I meant it. Faux Paw may not be much help, but trust me, she's a *big* distraction."

"You obviously got my note."

"Yes. And I came here—just as you knew I would—to tell you that you'll never figure out my sauce recipe, no matter how devious you are. So stop hinting that you know my secret ingredient. You don't."

He stepped aside and waved dramatically toward the living room. "My humble house is yours, fair lady. Please bring your suspicious mind and extremely ugly cat inside."

"Up, kitty."

Faux Paw twitched her tufted ears and rose to her three feet. A spider scurried across the doorsill. With a flick of one declawed front foot she scooped the spider to her mouth and ate it.

Max eyed her askance. "That was *my* dinner."

Betty never cracked a smile. She led Faux Paw inside and went to the couch. When she sat down, the cat leaned against her legs and scrubbed its head back and forth on her knees, its face contorted in one of the maniacal expressions which only cats can produce.

Betty had a very soft spot in her heart for this eccentric animal, Max decided. But then, he'd seen from the beginning that Betty treated the world and its inhabitants, both animal and human, with kindness. If she didn't extend that kindness to him, it was his own fault.

He rubbed his forehead wearily and settled in an armchair. "Lunch was very enlightening," he told her. "I haven't tasted barbecue that good since my grandfather made it. In fact, it was so good that it gave me a near-spiritual revelation. It raised a brief but very vivid memory. Of mushrooms."

"What a load of barbecued bull."

"You and my grandfather would have gotten along beautifully. He grew mushrooms in his cellar. Why don't you grow your mushrooms in your cellar instead of in a cave?"

"I like caves," she said emphatically, through gritted teeth. "I like mushrooms. I *don't* like you very much at the moment."

"What do you do with the mushrooms? They're not in the barbecue sauce—or if they are, they're chopped so fine that they can't be recognized."

"I'm not going to dignify this interrogation with answers."

"Hmmm. An interesting defense tactic. 'I refuse to answer on the grounds that it might incriminate me.' "

"I never thought that you'd stoop to scare tactics. What do you want to do—harrass me until I'm so addled that I fall into your arms?"

"Not a bad plan. But seriously, babe, I'm just trying to understand why *your* barbecue sauce brings back *my* childhood memories."

She raised a finger in warning. "If you're trying to say that your grandfather's recipe is the same as mine, you're mistaken."

"How can you be sure? Webster Springs is a small town, and fifty years ago it was even smaller. Our grandfathers were probably good friends."

"Not good enough to share the Quint-family barbecue recipe."

"Let's go see Norma. She would have been almost twenty back then. She might remember something."

"All right."

They stood. Max looked down at her somberly, seeing the anger in her eyes, but also the fear. It stabbed him with regret. "I'm not trying to hurt you, babe. But, frankly, I want to be with you, and if this is the only way I can get your attention, I'll take it."

Her eyes flickered with shock. Before she looked away, he was certain he saw confusion and tenderness in them. "Let's go visit Norma," she murmured, carefully keeping her gaze on Faux Paw.

Max wanted to take her in his arms and promise that he meant no harm to her or her silly secret about the barbecue sauce. Frustrated, he tapped a clenched hand against his leg and cleared his throat roughly. "Norma has two parakeets. The mutant cat won't try to turn them into appetizers, will she?"

Betty almost smiled. "Not unless they make spider sounds."

"What kind of sounds do spiders make?"

"Oh, no way, buddy. You'll have to *earn* the honor of hearing my incredible spider imitation. And at the rate you're going, you can forget it."

"You're a fascinating woman. Full of secrets. I intend to learn all of them."

"You're a fascinating man. Full of—"

"Save the compliments. Come along, Betty Belle." He gestured toward the front door.

"Maybe it wasn't going to be a compliment," she said with a fiendish smile.

Max was pleased with the smile, regardless of its origin. He laughed. "I suspected as much."

In her apartment above the wedding parlor Norma rocked in front of her fireplace with a section of quilt-piecing on her broad lap and a wary eye on Faux Paw, who lay below the parakeets' cage, whiskers twitching.

Betty hugged a loosely knitted wool shawl around her shoulders and sat on the edge of an upholstered chair. Again her gaze went to Max, who stood hip-shot by the fireplace, one arm stretched along the mantel, the other hand hooked over the waistband of his jeans.

He and Betty were respectfully waiting for Norma to answer their question. She was thinking. Betty met Max's eyes, and he shook his head slightly. She surmised that Norma didn't like to be interrupted when she was contemplating the past.

Betty glanced at a photograph on the mantel of a handsome young man wearing the marine dress uniform. Norma's son. Max's best friend. The bond of family between Max and Norma couldn't have been more obvious. He rested one big, lethal-looking hand on the back of Norma's chair with a gentleness that made Betty look away, fighting tears.

He had upset her earlier today and might do so again

before she left for home tonight. But she still wanted him. More than ever she sensed the rock-solid decency and compassion beneath his brashness.

"They had a falling out," Norma announced firmly. She stopped rocking and looked hard into Betty's eyes. "Your granddaddy and Max's. Yes, I do remember it. They were friends, but they quarreled over something. I know it because Ol' Mr. Quint used to let folks drive over the dirt road that ran across his property. It was a shortcut from the highway to town."

Betty was bewildered. "What road?"

"I remember it," Max interjected. "It was still there when I was a kid. But the forest was starting to take over. It's gone now." He looked at Norma curiously. "What did the road have to do with our grandfathers?"

"Ol' Mr. Quint closed it off. Blocked it with logs. Everybody got mad at him and didn't understand why he'd done it. All he'd say was that it was Mr. Templeton's fault. Mr. Quint never reopened the road, so I guess him and Mr. Templeton never settled their feud."

Betty and Max traded speculative looks. Max sat down on a footstool by Norma's chair and searched her solemn brown face intently. "Did you ever hear anyone talk about my grandpa's barbecue sauce?"

"My mama talked about it. She swore she was going to get the recipe out of him. She ran a little roadside stand every summer, and your granddaddy would barter quart jars of barbecue sauce for her vegetables."

"Did he ever give any hint about the ingredients?"

"Not that mama ever said. He guarded that recipe like nobody's business."

Max sighed and scrubbed a hand over his hair. "Well, I guess that's where the mystery dead-ends. If he was so worried about somebody stealing his recipe, he probably never wrote it down."

Betty breathed a sigh of relief and decided to be gracious in victory. "Then it certainly wasn't the same recipe that made *my* grandfather famous."

Norma gave her a puzzled stare. "Your granddaddy

wasn't famous for making barbecue sauce. Not that I know of, anyway. Max's granddaddy always entered his sauce in the county fair—and he always won first place with it. Don't you think your granddaddy would have entered his recipe if he'd had one?"

Betty wrapped her shawl tighter around her and awkwardly considered explanations. "Well, he must have been modest."

Max made a low growl of amusement. "Or a nervous thief."

Betty's chin snapped up. "Don't you dare—"

"Oh, don't get ruffled. I didn't mean it as a terrible insult. Swiping trade secrets is the American way, Betty Belle." He gave her a sardonic smile. "There's no law against copying a barbecue recipe. Or calling it your own. Or passing it along to your children and grandchildren. So that one of them can sell it. And make a lot of money. Hmmm?"

"Max, you're making accusations that aren't true and couldn't even be proved if they were. *My family recipe is no rip-off.*" She thumped her knee and shoved one foot forward, accidentally poking Faux Paw in the ribs. Faux Paw bounced up, startled, and knocked against the stand of the parakeets' cage.

The parakeets screeched. Norma yelped. The stand swayed. Max leapt up and grabbed it before it could fall. Betty vaulted from her chair, reaching for Faux Paw, who ducked her and collided with Max's legs. Max struggled to keep his balance and shoved the twenty-pound cat aside with his foot.

Seeing Faux's ears flatten viciously, Betty gasped. She sank her hands into the fur and loose skin of Faux Paw's neck just as the cat reared up and sank its defanged but still menacing teeth into Max's rump.

Faux Paw hung there, growling.

Max went very still. He couldn't maneuver in the cramped space between the bird-cage stand, the footstool, and the fireplace. He nobly kept his rescue hold

on the stand. Betty, horrified, jerked Faux Paw's collar, then grabbed the cat's jaw and tried to pry her loose.

"Faux won't hurt you!" she assured Max desperately. "Just be still! She doesn't like men. I think she's having a flashback to her first owner."

A muscle flexed in his jaw. Between gritted teeth he said slowly, "Please unhinge the future fur coat from my backside."

Betty finally pried Faux's jaw open and dragged the still-growling cat to a corner of the room, then knelt and wound an arm around Faux's neck.

She stared at Max's rump. A section of his jeans bore several tiny holes from Faux's teeth.

"Are you hurt?"

He didn't look pleased. He let go of the bird stand, smoothed a hand over his hip, and scowled. "How much sympathy is this worth?"

"I'll sew up the punctures in your jeans and buy you a bottle of rubbing alcohol."

"Will you do the rubbing?"

"No."

Norma, who had been watching in stunned silence, began to laugh in loud, gulping hoots. Betty stood shakily, wrapping a hand around Faux Paw's collar. "I think I'd better take Faux home. Good night, Norma. Thank you for the information."

Guffawing loudly, Norma could only manage to raise a hand in farewell while the other beat the arm of her rocking chair.

Max followed Betty downstairs and outside. They walked up the driveway to her van in silence. He didn't exactly limp, but he favored his bitten side. She chewed her lower lip both from tension and to keep from smiling. Faux Paw stalked along belligerently, straining at her leash.

When they reached the van, Betty put her in the front seat and hurriedly shut the door behind her. "I'm sorry, Max. Really."

Turning toward him in the light from his porch, she

tried to read his face. He looked at her with what seemed to be a combination of exasperation, amusement, and anger.

He raised a hand and cupped her chin. "You realize, of course, that this means war."

Her breath short, the hot, callused grip of his palm imprinting itself in her senses, she stepped back. "So what else is new? I've been under siege for weeks."

"Good night, babe. Get a lot of rest. You're going to need it."

She shook her head in disgust. "Idle threats."

She told herself not to worry. She was still telling herself when she got home. She was still worrying.

Max prowled the attic, limping, his hands clasped behind his back. God, what a bizarre evening. Life around Betty would probably always be surprising. The society babe and her mutant cat.

He halted and began to laugh, wondering how he must have looked with a deranged, three-footed cat hanging from his posterior. He glanced around the attic and silently said to hell with looking through more cookbooks. He had been grasping at straws. It wasn't funny, really, for a man of his dignity to use barbecue sauce for coercion, even gentle coercion.

He sat down on the couch and stared vaguely at the books that remained in the box. He missed Betty and wished he'd tried to talk her into coming inside for a drink. He should have used his injury to make her feel guilty. Max groaned in self-rebuke.

Dimly he noticed a book that seemed different from the rest. Looking closer, he frowned. An old Bible. Why would it be packed among the cookbooks? He lifted the thick black tome and gingerly opened it. Childhood memories of church services brought a warm feeling of pleasure to him. Immediately he decided to take the Bible downstairs and clean the musty cover. Perhaps

he'd even do a little reading. Stranger things had happened.

In the center of the Bible were several gilt-edged pages for recording family births, deaths, and marriages. Max was surprised and delighted to discover them. Reading the names, he gently turned from one page to the next.

The frail folded sheet of notepaper was tucked tightly into the Bible's crease. Max eased it out and spread it with his fingertips.

He read the recipe a half-dozen times, not believing it. Then he closed the Bible slowly and looked toward heaven. He winked and saluted. Someone up there was rooting for him . . . and Betty, it seemed.

Eight

Betty leaned in the doorway of the restaurant's veranda, adjusted the mounds of pink tulle and shiny silver rayon that comprised her fairy gown, and waved her magic wand at nothing in particular. She caught herself wishing for Max to appear. Where was he tonight? What was he wearing, thinking, eating, saying? Was he watching the evening star right now, as she was?

She let the wand droop. She adored the man. He filled her thoughts all the time, distracting her from her work, making her sleep badly at night, making her hold long one-sided conversations with Faux Paw about the consequences of blind, reckless devotion.

Behind her, the main door opened and several couples stepped out of the front hall. They smiled and commented on her costume. Betty studied their cheerful, satisfied expressions and concluded that they had enjoyed their dinners.

She idly watched them stroll across the lawn toward the parking lot. Perhaps Max would stop by for dinner sometime. Chiding herself for wanting to see him so badly, she tugged at her scratchy sequined bodice and tried to pay attention to the scene beyond the end of her street. From her place on the veranda, just a few

dozen yards from the square, she had a great view of the Halloween festivities.

Dusk was on the verge of becoming night. The shadows had just finished capturing the buildings. The weather was perfect—almost warm, the sky filling with stars, a light evening breeze lifting the rust-red leaves of the dogwoods that edged the park at the center of the square.

The merchants, who usually closed up shop by six-thirty, were all open late to host the local children for trick or treat. Main Street had been blocked off to traffic, and already costumed children were hurrying up the streets while their parents watched from benches along the sidewalks.

The scene made Betty's throat ache because it summed up so much that she loved about Webster Springs and so much that she wanted to share. It was so hokey and yet so perfect—the parents watching proudly, the children hurrying with excitement. Soon they would make their way to the shops and restaurants on the side streets, and Betty looked forward to greeting them.

Grace stepped out of the tiny house next door and waved merrily. Jack-o-lanterns and dried cornstalks adorned her shop's front porch. Grace was dressed as a queen bee, complete with cardboard-and-sequin crown, and antennae.

"You look majestic," Betty called.

"You look cute!" she called back. "You sparkle."

Betty shook her head. Flakes of glitter cascaded from her hair. "I overdid it. I itch. And I don't dare go back inside the restaurant. I'd get this 'fairy dust' everywhere. I'll have to stay out here with my food."

She gestured toward the floor, where a tall wicker basket sat, filled with homemade cookies wrapped in individual bags of black foil. The basket twinkled with tiny white lights. She'd propped the veranda's screened door open and strung lights around the opening, as well as along the rails on the steps, the azalea bushes that lined the front walk, and even the restaurant sign at the street.

Grace laughed. "Honey, what are you trying to do with all those lights? Draw moths?" She slapped her rounded bee-belly and answered her own question. "Yes! Handsome ol' boy moths! Well, send some of 'em over here!" She pivoted, her foam-stuffed stinger wiggling, and went back inside.

Betty smiled pensively. Boy moths. She waggled her wand. A familiar blue Jeep cruised up the back street and stopped by her curb. She nearly dropped her wand. *Be careful what you wish for. You might get it.*

Max swung his long legs out of the Jeep and stood with more casual aplomb—not to mention more pure sex appeal—than a man wearing fake buckskins and a raccoon cap ought to have. He gazed at her with equal surprise and stood motionless in the dramatic light of a Victorian-style street lamp.

Betty smiled at him blankly. She smoothed her dress with anxious fingers, then realized that there was no way to make herself look less ridiculous in a home-made fairy outfit with tulle bursting in every direction and glitter covering her face like a mask of shiny freckles.

Slowly he placed a hand over his heart. He sighed grandly, looking awestruck. His teasing attitude held an intensity that made her quiver with delight. He reached behind him, took the raccoon tail in one hand, and waved it at her. She gave him a droll once-over and poked her wand at him.

"Put your remote control away," he called. "You can't change my channel. You wouldn't really want to if you could read my mind."

She laughed, while desperation curled around her rib cage. They had to stop teasing each other, provoking each other.

"Meet my friend," he called. He went to the Jeep's passenger side and lifted a small child into his arms. Two small legs stuck out beneath a Batman cape. One leg was covered with denim and a tennis shoe. The other was covered in a bulky white cast.

Betty watched in puzzled silence as Max carried the

little boy up the front walk. Max held the child carefully in the crook of one powerful arm. The boy clutched a trick-or-treat bag and stared at Betty through a slightly skewed Batman mask, his mouth open in wonder.

"What are *you*?" he asked.

"I'm the cookie fairy. Welcome to my home." She waved the wand, then pulled a pinch of glitter from a concealed pocket in her skirt and tossed it into the air.

Max carried him up the steps as Betty moved back, her gaze moving from the child to Max's riveting, approving eyes. He set the child in front of her, then cupped a brawny hand under the boy's elbow, supporting him. "This is Christopher. He lives with his grandmother, and she's not feeling good tonight. So he and I are a team."

Betty knelt by the child. "You make a very handsome team."

"Max is gonna teach me how to burp loud."

"Oh?" Betty cocked her head. "I'm sure he's wonderful at burping."

"Yeah! Do one, Max! Go ahead! Show her!"

"I don't think girls like that kind of thing."

Betty huffed in mild disgust. "What arrogance. I was the best burper at my elementary school."

She and Max traded private smiles. He threw his head back and laughed. "I should have known."

"I want to hear you burp, please," Christopher said to her.

Still laughing, Max patted the boy on the shoulder. "I don't think we'd better encourage her. She probably practices all the time. Maybe later, okay? Besides, you and I have a lot of trick-or-treating to do right now."

"Oh, yeah! Okay!" The child grinned up at him, and he grinned back.

Betty glowed. Was this the same man who'd said that he didn't care about having a family? The careful, unhurried way he treated the boy told her that this retired marine major could be a major teddy bear. Interesting.

"Trick or treat," Christopher said shyly, holding out his bag.

"Treat." She reached into the wicker basket and retrieved three shiny black packets. "Here are two home-made chocolate-chip cookies for you." She put them in Christopher's bag.

"Remember what I told you to say?" Max prompted, nudging his arm.

"Thank you, ma'am."

For some absurd reason she had tears behind her eyes. "You're welcome, Christopher." Betty stood and handed the third cookie to Max. "You get a treat too, Daniel Boone."

He smiled at her, his expression indicating that he had better treats in mind. They gazed at each other wordlessly. Christopher tugged at Max's buckskin britches. Betty looked down finally. Christopher was trying very hard, through contorted expressions and a secretive nod in her direction, to convey a message to Max.

"Oh! Pardon me," Max said solemnly. He looked at his cookie packet, then at Betty. "Thank you very much, cookie fairy."

Christopher nodded, obviously satisfied. She wanted to laugh, giggle, cry a little, and follow the two of them on the rest of their rounds. Enjoying Max and Christopher would have been her private Halloween treat. She stifled her impulses and merely smiled. "You're welcome, Daniel Boone."

At the first station across the square, sirens began to wail. Betty jumped.

"A fire!" Christopher squealed in excitement.

Max stepped to the edge of the veranda, watching as all three of the town's engines pulled out of the red-brick station. They crept down the street until they exited the square. Then they picked up speed quickly and roared out of sight.

"They're headed south," Max noted. He shrugged. "Probably just a brushfire. Somebody must have been burning trash and set their backyard on fire."

The door to the house swung open. Betty pivoted as Andy burst out, waving his hands at her. "The sheriff just called. Your house is on fire!"

For a horrified moment Betty stared at him in disbelief. Then she swung toward Max, knowing without hesitation that he would help her. "My cat! Faux Paw is in the house!"

"Let's go." He lifted Christopher and handed him to Andy. "Can you see that Batman gets to finish trick-or-treating?"

"Sure." Andy lifted the mask and peered at him. "Hello, Christopher."

"And then get him home to his grandmother," Betty added. Her mind was numb. She patted the child's hand, then left the veranda at a run.

She was halfway across the lawn when Max caught up with her. He ran ahead of her to the Jeep and swung the door open, then scooped her up and tossed her inside.

"Take it easy, babe. Nothing's going to happen to the mutant cat."

She nodded calmly, but hugged herself hard. She could lose Faux Paw and her house. Her *home.* The night suddenly seemed full of evil that was very real, and very close.

By the time she and Max arrived, flames were leaping from the upper rooms. The fire trucks sat on the lawn, and long streams of water arched from their hoses, held by calm-faced men with cheeks full of chewing tobacco. Judging by the crowd behind the firemen, most of her neighbors had come to watch the spectacle.

Sick fear washed over Betty as Max guided the Jeep through a pack of cars and trucks. She shoved her door open and leapt out while the Jeep was still rolling, dimly hearing—and ignoring—Max's stern call to wait and his harried curses when she didn't.

She dodged through the parked vehicles and then the crowd, her pink ballet shoes slipping treacherously on the water-soaked grass. At the edge of the crowd

she stepped in a cold puddle and fell. Several people helped her to her feet but blocked her way.

She groaned in defeat and strained to see her house. The front door stood open. Two firemen trotted out, axes in hand. They shook their heads and motioned to the others to stay away.

"Did you see my cat?" she yelled to them.

The roar of the fire prevented them from hearing her. Betty waited for her neighbors to look away; when they did, she bolted past them. She didn't get far. A large, hard hand clamped onto her forearm. She felt like a small puppy hitting the end of a strong leash. She swung about fiercely.

"Stop it! I'm going in the house!"

"You're not going anywhere," Max ordered, scowling down at her. He'd tossed the raccoon cap. In the firelight his face was harsh and worried. He jabbed a finger downward. "Your life's worth more than a cat's. Stay here. I'll go."

A different kind of fear surged up in her chest. She grabbed his fringed leather shirt. "No! No! Max, I can call her! If she's hiding downstairs, she'll come to me! I don't want you to go in there!"

He picked her up and shoved her into the grip of a burly old farmer and his equally burly wife. "Y'all hold her by the ears if you have to."

"Now, Miss Betty, you just calm down, calm down—"

"Max! Don't go in there! Max!" She struggled uselessly, her eyes never leaving Max as he ran through the haze of water, floodlights, and firelight. He ducked through the front door while a half-dozen firemen ran after him, shouting and waving their arms.

They followed him unhappily into the house. With a dull boom the upper story collapsed on itself. Sparks, smoke, and flames billowed in all directions. The house's lower level trembled. The firemen immediately ran back outside. Max didn't.

Betty clawed at the hands that held her. "Max! Come out! Max!" The second-story floor crumbled on one

side, dumping timbers into the kitchen below. The kitchen windows shattered and smoke poured out. Burning wood hissed ominously as the firemen hosed it down, sending clouds of mist into the air.

Betty's throat hurt. She was screaming silently, watching what remained of her home begin to lurch to the right like a child's doll house being flattened by a playful hand. She didn't think about the house. She didn't think about Faux Paw. She thought about Max. There were several people holding her in place now, because she was struggling wildly to get free.

The house groaned as hundreds of nails ripped from the old boards. The lower level toppled sideways. The porch collapsed with a deafening whoosh. Its tin roof screamed.

Betty slid to the ground in a heap and buried her face in her hands. *Max, I love you. I love you.*

"Look!" someone bellowed. "There he is!"

She scrambled to her feet and nearly climbed the back of the man in front of her. Max staggered through the backyard. He swayed. Faux Paw was draped over his shoulder.

Everyone forgot Betty and ran toward him. Laughing, crying, she barely noticed when she fell down twice during her own mad rush to get to him.

He sank to the ground, holding Faux Paw around the haunches. The cat's head hung down the front of his torso. She was limp. He slapped her on the back, and she began to cough. Betty pushed through the circle of people and tumbled to her knees in front of him.

She couldn't speak. All she could do was laugh in a gulping, slightly hysterical way as she ran her hands over him and Faux Paw. He was covered in grime, and smoke rose from the black patches on his shirt and britches.

He was gasping for breath, but he finally managed to speak. "I smell . . . like bad . . . barbecue."

"You smell *wonderful*." She grasped his face between both hands and kissed him. Faux Paw coughed louder

and began shaking her head. Betty stroked the old cat anxiously. Faux Paw drew several deep breaths and started wiggling.

"Here." Max pulled her from his shoulder. Betty sat cross-legged beside him and they stretched the cat across their laps. A fireman brought a bottle of oxygen and held the mask over Faux Paw's muzzle. After a few seconds of heavy breathing she raised her head and hissed at the world in general.

"Alive and still sweet," Max noted.

With one hand Betty caressed Faux Paw's dirty, singed fur. She slid the other hand around Max's waist, then leaned against him. He quickly put an arm around her shoulders and held her so tightly that she felt like asking for an oxygen mask herself. She didn't mind a bit. "How did you get out of the house?"

"I didn't spend twenty years in the marines for nothing," he said solemnly. "I'm trained to use every resource in a dangerous situation. I react with finely honed skills in an emergency, not to mention superior intelligence and physical perfection."

"So how'd you get out of the house?" a bystander asked eagerly.

"The back door was unlocked."

People guffawed and applauded. Betty rested her head on his shoulder and shut her eyes. She felt his arm squeezing her, and she stroked his back with ragged, thankful little motions of her hand.

The fire chief broke through the crowd and knelt in front of her. She looked at him wearily. "Thank you. I know that you and your men did everything that you could."

He nodded. "I sure am sorry. Looks like the fire started in the upstairs bedroom."

"I left an electric floor heater turned on. But it was supposed to be one of the safest models on the market."

"The wiring in your house was so old, no telling what happened. But it's a good bet that the heater caused an overload."

"But you have insurance, of course," Max interjected.

Betty stared at the smoking remnants of what was to have been her dream home. It began to hit her—she'd just watched the destruction of a Quint family legacy. She was almost broke, and now her home was gone, along with most of her belongings.

"I just moved my furniture in last week," she murmured.

"Babe? Your insurance?" Max repeated.

Betty looked at him grimly. "Never buy cheap homeowner's insurance from a small company, Maximilian."

"What are you saying?"

"My insurance company declared bankruptcy last month. I hadn't gotten around to buying a new policy yet."

"Oh, babe. I'm so sorry." Max shut his eyes. When he opened them, they were sympathetic, but puzzled. She could imagine what he wanted to ask. Why cheap insurance? Why delay in replacing it? And why hadn't she begun remodeling, as she'd said she was planning to do?

The fire chief shook his head sadly and moved away. People drifted toward their vehicles. The firemen spat tobacco and chatted while they continued dousing the remnants of the fire.

Feeling shell-shocked, Betty stroked Faux Paw's head and looked up at Max, communicating with him through haunted eyes. "Thank God you're all right," she whispered finally. "That's all I really care about at the moment. I don't want to talk about the house just now."

He cupped the back of her head and brought her close for a kiss. "Care to stay in my guest room for a few days? I've never had a beautiful, muddy, pink fairy as a house guest before. Or a mutant cat that is now gnawing on the hand that saved its life."

Betty looked down. Faux Paw was chewing lightly on Max's fingers. But then she gave them a loving swipe with her tongue and rubbed her head on his knee. "She's crazy about you. She'll probably follow you around from now on. I don't think she can resist anymore."

"You sound certain," he said carefully.

Betty raised her head and met Max's warm, searching green eyes. "Because I know exactly how she feels."

Max glanced at a small digital clock on the mantel over the fireplace. Three A.M. He rubbed his forehead wearily, feeling the strain of the evening's events—not the fire, but its effect on Betty. He had never felt so much anxiety or such tenderness before, and he'd spent the past few hours pouring all of his energy into making her feel better.

He wasn't certain what he'd accomplished. She had eaten a sandwich at his insistence. She'd had a glass of cognac. She'd allowed herself to cry inside the comfort of his arms as he and she had sat on the couch in the dark. But she hadn't wanted to talk, to answer the questions that he wanted to ask, that she must know he wanted answered.

When he'd mentioned that she ought to call her parents, she had shaken her head. They were in Europe. Her mother would overreact and her father would make scolding comments about the electric heater. Betty had told him, with a thin little smile, that her parents' sympathy could be hard on the nerves.

So Max offered silent support. Inside himself he found something he thought he'd lost forever. He found a willingness to accept her silence, her mystery. He found a faith in her and because of her.

"Max?" Her soft voice came to him from the hallway. He turned swiftly and looked at her. She stood there with one of his large white bath towels in her hands. Her hair was still damp from her shower. It wisped around her face and neck in gleaming black strands, giving her a disheveled, vulnerable look.

Rings of fatigue circled her eyes, but she smiled as she glanced down at herself. She wore a set of his gray sweats. The shirt hung halfway to her knees, and the pants were so baggy and so long that they draped in

big folds around her ankles. "I've been swallowed. I could rent space in this for conventions."

"I'll call Norma and see if she can find—"

"No." Her eyes moved over him with disarming affection. "I like wearing this. It's fine." Studying him further, she frowned. "You look exhausted. Go take a shower yourself."

He nodded, loving her concern, trying gruffly not to let her see how much he wished that they'd taken a shower together. He rose and went to her. They walked down the hall, and he followed her into the guest room, where Faux Paw lay snoring in the center of the bed.

Max didn't want to think about sleeping in his own room alone, but he wasn't sure how Betty would react if he suggested otherwise. He doubted that she'd believe him if he said that comfort and closeness were uppermost in his mind.

He brushed his lips over her forehead, then stepped back brusquely. "Good night, babe. Sleep well."

She started to say something, caught herself, and simply nodded. Max couldn't decipher the mysterious gleam in her eyes, but it was too provocative for his current emotional state, so he gave her a friendly wink and left the room.

Thirty minutes later he dragged himself from a shower that he'd alternately run hot and cold, trying to relax at the same time that every thought and impulse begged for Betty. He would have been satisfied with just holding her, an attitude that he analyzed with surprise, hardly believing it himself.

Toweling his hair, his body feeling cool and exhausted inside blue pajama bottoms and a thick blue robe, he walked down the hall and entered his bedroom. He halted in the darkness, staring at the bed, wondering for a second if the shadowy light from the hallway was playing tricks on him.

Betty was asleep on his futon, curled up on her side with his burgundy quilt and sheet pulled over her, and both hands curled under her chin. Max dropped his

towel and padded quietly to her side. The futon was cushioned by a mattress and also sat atop a mahogany platform he'd built for it; still, it was low to the floor.

He knelt by it and touched her cheek with the back of his fingers. *There won't be any reprieve the next time,* he'd warned. But now he said gently, "Betty Belle. You may be in the wrong bed. It depends on why you're here."

She struggled awake, smiled at him groggily, then reached out and stroked her fingers along his jaw. "I know you're exhausted, but would you mind if I slept with you? I really want to stay close to you."

After a moment he cleared his throat. "No problem." He suppressed an urge to smile broadly and grab her in a hug. Max tossed his robe and climbed into bed behind her.

She turned to face him and gently laid her palms on his chest. "I'm so tired. I can barely keep my eyes open."

"Me either."

Max felt serenity slip through him at her touch; a peaceful brand of arousal let him settle his head on the pillow and pull her to him without hurry, knowing that he'd never shared such perfect friendship and comfort. The insistent hardness against his belly lost its urgency. He would never be too tired to want her, but for now the anticipation was sweet satisfaction in itself.

She nuzzled her face into the center of his chest. With the ease of complete trust they arranged themselves in a snug, comfortable embrace, legs entwined, arms draped loosely over each other's sides, faces burrowed together above the quilt's edge.

"Oh, Max," she whispered, her voice fading but filled with contentment. "You were wonderful tonight. I'll never forget it."

He chuckled against her hair. "I won't let you."

Betty tiptoed back into the bedroom after checking on Faux Paw. She stopped by a window only a few feet

from the big futon and let her eyes adjust to the starlight. The slightest hint of dawn lightened the patch of sky between the valance and the bottom panels of the window's simple white curtains. She anxiously watched Max sleep.

She'd been so groggy, so ready to fall asleep as soon as his arms were around her, that only now did she realize how she'd taken advantage of him. She recalled everything about his body, including the hard ridge of his arousal brushing against her thigh as she had snuggled mindlessly against him, using him for her own comfort.

He had needed more. She had expected him to say so. But he hadn't. Instead he'd sighed so happily that she'd fallen asleep in a blissful dream. This man was incredibly special. He was honest with her, and she'd be honest with herself. She belonged to him in a way that she would never belong to any other man.

Max, who lay on his back, seemed to realize that she was gone from bed. He stirred and sleepily stretched a hand out, searching for her. Tenderness and desire heated her blood. Smiling, she stripped off the bulky sweat suit. She went to the futon and slipped under the covers.

She nestled close to him without letting her body touch his. Slowly she placed her hands on his bare shoulders. A soft, half-awake sound of pleasure rumbled from his throat. Betty quivered with anticipation and pulled herself near enough to brush kisses across his parted lips. He sleepily wrapped his arms around her and dragged her against him.

His whole body tensed. Instantly awake, he shoved himself up on one elbow. "Max," she whispered, drawing her hand down the softly furred muscles of his chest. "No regrets, Max. We need each other in so many ways."

Above her he was a large, potently masculine form of shadow and warm, musky scent. His hair was ruffled in a way that made her hands anxious to stroke it,

then ruffle it again. His eyes were hooded from sleep, but weren't sleepy. Her breath drew short as she measured the sexual energy leashed in his motionless scrutiny.

"I'll do my best to make you happier than you've ever been before," he promised in a low, gravelly voice.

"I'll return the favor."

He took the edge of the covers, and she quivered as his fingertips trailed across the tops of her breasts. By intimate degrees he drew the covers back. His gaze caressed her, creating almost tangible sensations on her skin and deep inside her womb. Her back arched instinctively; her legs shifted against his, and her breasts ached for his touch.

Pulling the covers down further, he traced her navel with his thumb, then pressed a knuckle into the soft indentation and rubbed gently. Trickles of exquisite desire ran through her belly. She grasped his shoulders as he molded his hand to her stomach and began to stroke the supersensitive skin. His hand moved upward.

"Great ribs. I suspected it," he teased hoarsely. "And look what I found on top of them."

Betty moaned as his hand moved over her breast. The air seemed to hum with expectation. The heat from their bodies mingled with the earthy fragrance of arousal. There would be nothing inhibited about their lovemaking; no coy games, no holding back.

With an abrupt, ragged sigh, his restraint failed him and he scooped his arms under her. Betty cupped his face as he crushed her to the bed, and their mouths met in a sweet but frantic search for satisfaction.

She stroked her hands over his shoulders and back, skimming the flexing muscles, then raising her hands to his hair, sliding her fingers into it. It was like short, luxurious mink, contrasting delightfully with the coarser hair of his body. She continued her explorations, reveling in the changing shapes, angles, and textures she found. Her fingertips danced over his jaws, loving the play of the sinews as his skillful, inventive mouth moved

against hers. She cupped his heavyset shoulders and slid her hands down his arms, pausing at small, puckered spots that puzzled her. She had felt similar marks on his back.

"Shrapnel scars," he whispered hastily. "From 'Nam. They're not as noticeable as they feel to the touch."

A soft, anguished protest burst from her throat. "They're fine. Fine. I don't mind them at all." She kissed him and was rewarded with his smile against her lips.

He dragged his hands down her spine and under her hips, squeezing their round pads erotically, then curving his fingers under her thighs, tantalizing her.

Betty writhed upward, seeking the hard plane of his belly and finding the straight, thick ridge of his sex through the thin pajama bottoms he wore. She tucked her hands between their bodies and fumbled with the pajamas' tie string. It was secured with a tight knot. "Max, what did you do to this?" she asked in dismay. "Is this an anti-invasion device?"

Chuckling gruffly, he sat back and unfastened the cord. "I was trying to protect you from a military secret."

He lifted his hands. The waistband of his pajama bottoms sagged loosely, revealing his navel and a swath of the lean, hairy abdomen beneath it. Betty sat up and clasped his waist, drawing her palms down his sides.

She tilted her head back so that she could watch his expression. "Perhaps I should lower your defenses, Major."

Max took her face between his hands. His thumbs stroked her cheeks gently. "I surrender."

Trembling with love and desire, Betty pulled the pajamas to his thighs. Studying him breathlessly, she thought of no words that could do him justice. Mewling her appreciation instead, she leaned down and kissed his straining body.

"You're generous . . . in victory." He tried to joke, but the words faded into a low sigh.

She stroked his thighs. "Lay down and let me show you how generous."

He settled on his back and watched her in electric silence. The short, quick rhythm of his breathing matched her own. She knelt beside him as she eased the thin cotton pajamas down his legs and over his feet.

Betty noticed the left foot and bit her lip to keep from crying out. She ran her fingertips over the surface scars, then touched the area where his little toe had been.

He cleared his throat and murmured, "That piggy went to market."

She laughed shakily, then bent and gave the spot a kiss. "Poor thing."

His voice became a roughly grained purl, as provocative as a caress. "Do you know how incredible you look, sitting there naked?"

She heard herself make a trill of pleasure. It was so birdlike that both she and Max broke into low, private laughter, sharing a joy that erased the sadness of a second earlier. He held out both hands and she went to him swiftly, lowering herself atop him and trilling again, this time in unison with his husky murmur of delight.

Now each kiss was slow and thorough, meant to ignite slow writhing movements and complement the new journeys of their hands. He curved his down her hips and thighs, then delved into her with careful, unhurried fingers. His light, almost teasing strokes brought her to a level of dazed bliss.

"You make me feel as if I'm perfect," she told him, knowing that she was returning his urgent, desire-drugged gaze. "Or that parts of me are perfect, at least."

He shuddered and laughed hoarsely. His hips rotated between her thighs, gently grinding his length against the downy center in a way that made her body throb. "All of your parts are fantastic. My parts are crazy about them. And the *sum* of our parts—"

"Feels like this." She slid herself onto him, smoothly, quickly, calling his name.

His body bowed in startled response, and his hands

dug into her hips. Throwing his head back, he shut his eyes and cursed joyfully, his tone as tender as a love poem. When he shot her an apologetic look, Betty smiled and shook her head at him. "Point accepted," she whispered. "Well said, Major."

His eyes gleamed. He wrapped his arms around her. In one powerful movement he rolled her onto her back, their bodies still intimately merged, his thrusting even deeper. The commanding ache inside her belly began to grow into a storm that couldn't be contained. She held Max tightly and whispered against his ear, "Take us there, Max. Take us there."

He kissed her until neither of them had breath or control or concentration enough to do anything except make the fast, sweet trip home.

Nine

Coming home to Betty felt right. In fact, after just a few days, it felt not only right but essential. Max had never been happier with the fact that Webster Springs needed only a part-time magistrate. The afternoon stretched ahead, waiting to turn his anticipation into all sorts of delights.

"Where's my woman?" he bellowed cheerfully, striding into the house and slamming the front door behind him.

She staggered out of the bedroom and grinned at him. She was nearly hidden behind an enormous armload of clothes. All he could see of her were her head, arms, and bare feet. "I just got back from Atlanta. Look! I have clothes again. You can take the Daisy Mae outfit back to the parlor."

"Damn. That was my favorite costume. And it had great accesories. A white shotgun for the father of the bride to carry."

From behind the mountain of clothes she made a mild sound of disgust. "I should have retired that costume for good."

He strolled toward her, smiling drolly, calculating just how long it would be before they were in bed. "Babe, I'm glad that you had clothes in storage down in

Atlanta, and I know that you've been traumatized by the fire, but you don't have to clutch what's left of your possessions for safekeeping. I'll give you closet space. You look like an ant trying to wrestle a cotton ball."

"Oh? What do I look like now?" She dropped the clothes. She was wearing only a pair of sheer black panties.

Max vaulted to her and swung her up in his arms. "You look like a woman who's about to be kissed, fondled, and—"

"I knew you'd get the point." Laughing, she unfastened his string tie and shirt collar, then nuzzled her lips to his throat. Her voice became husky and serious. "I thought you'd *never* get here."

He trembled as he carried her to bed. Once there he made her tremble along with him. It was good to be home. It was good to know that home meant Betty. When he was deep inside her, holding her, losing control to the sounds of her moans, he knew that home would never be the same if he lost her. It was a sobering thought.

In the quiet aftermath, she sensed his change of mood. Raising her head from his shoulder, she stroked a strand of damp hair from his temple and smiled at him curiously. "What are you thinking about so hard?"

Max cupped her face in one hand and studied the loving gray eyes, the generous mouth, the unconventional beauty of her angular, imperfect features. "You're unique and wonderful. That's what I'm thinking."

"Such good taste you have."

"You're awfully quiet yourself. And you look pale. How do you feel?"

She idly stroked the matted brown hair of his chest, then rested her hand there and propped her chin on it. "I keep thinking about my house. And trying to decide what to do next."

"That's simple. You're going to live with me now."

"Not for long." She raised her head and looked at

him gently. "I tried that with someone once before, Max. It's not my style."

"I thought we'd gotten beyond that problem. It's not a question of respect, or caring, or commitment. We have all that, don't we?"

"Yes. Yes, we do. I didn't say that I wanted to stop seeing you." She hesitated, frowned as if wrestling with a private decision, then looked at him closely. "I . . . uhmmm. I have to be honest . . . damn. I don't want to be. But I owe it to you."

She bowed her head to his chest for a second, and he felt the tension coursing through her, her leg tightening as it lay across his thighs, her torso feeling stiff against his side.

"Just say it," he urged softly, stroking her back.

She met his eyes and nodded. "I still intend to marry and have a family. I'll give you time, but I won't give that up." She put a fingertip over his lips as he started to speak. "That's not a threat, Max; that's simply a fact."

She drew her hand away and waited for his response. Confusion surged through him, along with bittersweet frustration. "I'm not asking you to give up anything. I think we have it all."

"No." She rose and went to the pile of clothes in the hallway. She found a shimmering silver robe and belted it around herself as she walked back to the bed. Max pulled the quilt over himself and sat up, watching her body glide under the sheer material, watching the way her chin lifted and her shoulders squared.

She stopped at the foot of the bed and looked at him with a mixture of dignity and sadness. The combination sent shivers of emotion up his spine.

"I love you," she murmured, as if it hurt her to say it. "I love you dearly."

He drew a ragged breath. "I love you too. Like I've never loved anyone before. Do you believe me when I say that?"

She nodded. "That's what makes all of this so painful. And so fantastic. And so frightening."

"And so simple." He held out his hands. She knelt beside him and clasped them in her lap. "Let's give it time," he whispered. "Let's live for each other and each day."

"All right. For now. I'll do anything to be with you. That's what you've coaxed from me, Max. Total devotion."

"It's not one-sided," he murmured, bringing her hands to his mouth and kissing them. "I'm not your wishy-washy musician."

"I knew that weeks ago," she agreed with a slight nod and a rueful smile. "Don't say it that way. He's not mine—I don't claim him. I don't want to claim him. I don't even want to remember him. I just want to remember what I promised myself because of him."

Max drew her down beside him and held her possessively. He looked at her flushed, sorrowful face and knew that he'd have to sort out his tangled feelings about marriage, for her sake. It was a task he dreaded. "Do you know how *much* I love you?" he asked gruffly.

A poignant but mischievous gleam entered her eyes. "Show me."

He did. Trust and confidence flared between them, but later she looked at him with unabashed challenge in her eyes. He returned the look in full.

She didn't like the way he smiled at her when she finally let him board the bus. He smiled as if he knew a secret, but her stern scrutiny only made him laugh. "God, that barbecue sauce smells good! And the sun feels wonderful! And I'm with you! What a great Saturday!"

He slapped his chest, which was covered in a plaid flannel shirt. Leather suspenders pulled snug across the handsome expanse as he stretched languidly. He

wore brown corduroy trousers and soft leather hiking shoes. "I'm ready to play caterer," he announced.

Betty adopted a nonchalant facade. "You're certainly homey and comfortable looking." *As if homey and comfortable ever looked so marvelous,* she added silently. He held her dreams in the palm of his brawny hand. It wouldn't do to praise him too much.

He looked around the bus and inhaled deeply. "It really smells fantastic. The sauce is finished, I presume?"

"All done." She opened a cooler and pointed to a neat row of gallon jars. "When we get to the country club, we'll just slap the ribs on my trusty portable grill and start spreading the sauce over them."

He held out his hands and looked at them solemnly. "I have chapped skin. I never spent an entire Friday evening making coleslaw before. I must have washed a thousand heads of cabbage."

She cleared her throat and tugged brusquely at the bright print sweater that topped her jeans. Then she swaggered up to him and tapped his chest with an imperious finger. "As I recall, you were easily distracted from making coleslaw. In fact, you spent quite a lot of time on other pursuits."

"I couldn't help myself. Watching you knead biscuit dough was too enticing." He lifted her by the elbows and kissed her thoroughly. When he set her back down, she leaned against him, chuckling. *Admit it, Betty Belle. No matter how footloose he may be, you're blissfully happy with this man.*

"Thank you for helping me," she murmured, hugging him.

He slipped his arms around her and held her snugly. "This much happiness ought to be illegal. Or at least immoral."

"You may not be so cheerful by the end of the day."

"We'll come home and take a long, hot bath."

"Hmmm." She moved away from him and busied herself checking supplies that were packed neatly in bins along one wall. She could feel him watching her. "Yes?"

"If this is so much work, why don't you hire a couple of people to help you with it? You told me that you used to have assistants."

"I'm trying to simplify my operations. Streamline. Be efficient." *And I don't have the money to hire anyone right now.* She straightened and saluted him playfully. "You should approve, Major."

"I just don't understand. With all the money you make—"

She came to him and stopped his questions with a slow, tantalizing kiss. "The only problem I have, dear sir, is that we're going to be late to a very well-paying job if we don't get moving." She stroked his shoulders and fluttered her eyelashes at him. "Would you drive this big ol' bus for little ol' me? I declare, I don't know how I managed before you came along."

His eyes danced with amusement. "Uh huh. I recognize a steel magnolia trying to masquerade as a wilting lily."

"Why, the insult!"

He slapped her lightly on the rump, stepped back, and bowed. "I'll drive your bus, Miss Betty," he drawled. "And I'll protect your secret barbecue sauce faithfully. I won't even mention the fact that I could be trusted with the secret."

She laughed, but felt guilty. She *could* trust Max. It was wrong not to tell him. But there was something mysterious about his smile, and something just a little unnerving about his confidence. Betty winked at him. "If you're good, maybe someday I'll give you the recipe."

As an engagement gift.

What made her work so hard? Max wearily tilted his head back on the driver's seat as he guided the bus

through the darkness toward his house. He glanced over his shoulder. Betty was asleep, exhausted. She lay curled up on one of the cushioned benches of the small dining booth that sat directly behind his seat.

She ought to hire at least two helpers for these jobs. Even with him to assist her, the work load had been enormous. They'd fed four hundred people. Max would be happy if he never saw a plate of barbecue again.

On the other hand, he'd had fun. And he'd loved the sense of partnership. He had even loved the prim way she ignored him when he gave her orders. Without being blunt about it, she made him realize that his communication skills needed work, at least around civilians. But she also made it clear that she loved having him with her, and that she needed him.

Max sat forward in the driver's seat and scowled. Several guests, interested in having events of their own catered, had come to him and Betty asking questions about scheduling and costs. They'd assumed that he and she were married. She had politely explained that they weren't.

And Max had felt regret. Regret. He rapped his fingers on the steering wheel. Was it because he disliked any situation that made Betty unhappy—that he simply preferred to avoid a subject on which they disagreed? Or was it some subtle shift in his attitude? No. Consider marriage? Him? Never!

Betty stretched, yawned, and sat up. She got to her knees behind him and lightly draped her arms around his neck. Her sleepy, seductive voice tickled his ear. "Driver, do you ever cavort with your passengers?"

He was relieved by the distraction. This was reality, and it was damned sweet. He had all the love in the world right here, right now. "Ma'am, it depends on the kind of ticket you bought. Do you want to go all the way?"

"Oh, yes."

They shared a low chuckle. She kissed his cheek. "Let me take over. I'll drive. You rest."

"Good timing. We're about a mile from my house."

"Oh, Max. I'm so sorry. I didn't mean to let you—"

"Sssh. You earned the sleep. It was a long day."

"It was nice having you with me. Not just for the help but for the sharing. I've never had that before." She put her head on his shoulder, and after a second he realized that she was dozing. Her hands lay gently on his chest, open and vulnerable. Her breath caressed his cheek.

Max stared straight ahead, his teeth clenched. He couldn't help thinking, *Betty Templeton. It has a nice ring to it.*

Betty sat at a desk in her bare, practical little office at the back of the restaurant. Peering at a computer screen, she studied the accounts from the first three weeks of operation and was very pleased. There wouldn't be any profit for a while, but she'd expected that. Business was going better than her projections, which had been conservative.

She rested her head on one hand. Given a little extra cash, she could begin bottling the barbecue sauce for distribution locally. Betty sighed, then turned the computer off. There would be no extra cash for a long, long time. Right now she'd have to be satisfied with selling the sauce from a display shelf up by the cashier's stand.

A herd of footsteps clumped on the wooden floor outside her open door. She looked up as three excited waitresses filled the opening. "You have to come to the front," one of them told her. "A man's asking for you."

"And he just bought every bottle of barbecue sauce that we had! Fifty bottles!"

"And he had his *chauffeur* come inside and get them!"

"His limousine is parked right on the street!"

"He ate pork barbecue and left me a ten-dollar tip!"

Betty bolted to her feet. "I can't wait to see this amazing customer for myself."

The waitresses followed her through the back hall and into the kitchen. "He's so handsome! And so unusual looking!"

"He has white hair! Silver-white. But he's not old."

Andy glared at them from behind a serving rack. "He looks foreign to me."

"He's not foreign. He's southern."

Intrigued, Betty stepped out of the hall behind the cashier's stand. The man who waited patiently was, indeed, cause for scrutiny. Because of the white hair he made her think of an elegant swan, though the image failed to capture the rugged quality about him. Few men could wear a double-breasted suit of gray pinstripes and not look boring. This man's suit had a European cut that emphasized his body, and his body was definitely not boring.

"May I help you?" Betty asked pleasantly, stopping in front of him.

He smiled with great charm, but his eyes, under dramatic white brows, had a shrewdness that chilled her. "Ms. Quint, I'm very pleased to meet you. My name is T. S. Audubon. I'm an old friend of Max Templeton's."

"Ah." She smiled and shook the large, graceful hand he extended. "If you're looking for Max, he's—"

"Oh, no. I came here today to meet you. To speak with you about Max. More precisely, about his career, and your relationship to it."

Bewildered, she studied the visitor in silence. An ominous feeling grew inside her chest. This man obviously knew a great deal about her and Max, and he didn't look pleased about it.

She lifted her chin. "Please, come to my office." She made a vague gesture toward the back of the restau-

rant while she continued to watch him. "This sounds interesting."

The mysterious T. S. Audubon smiled thinly. "I suspect that you won't choose such a mild adjective after you hear what I have to say."

It was odd for Betty to stay at the restaurant so late. Max knew that she was intense about her work, but she had confidence in Andy and usually left the restaurant by six each night.

He kept worrying about her and had trouble concentrating on the wedding ceremony. This was such a grand one too. The bride and groom had brought their own costumes. In honor of Thanksgiving, a few days away, both were dressed as pilgrims. The parlor was packed with the couple's relatives and friends. Some were dressed as Pilgrims. A couple were dressed as Indians. None was dressed as a turkey, which disappointed Max. It would have been a first.

Afterward, Norma supervised a reception that featured pumpkin cake. Max put in an appearance, signed the wedding certificate, then slipped out to the veranda, where he paced in the cold darkness, watching the road.

A short while later Norma followed him. "I heard some folks talking in there," she told him. "They saw a stranger in town today. A strange stranger—how many visitors come to Webster Springs in a limousine?"

Max pivoted toward her, instantly alert. "And?"

"White haired, but youngish. Tall. Good-looking and fancy dressed. He had lunch at Betty's place."

Max was stunned. "Damn him."

Norma grunted in agreement. "That sneaky Audubon. He's goin' to cause you trouble, son. If he hasn't already."

A vehicle swept up the road and pulled into the driveway of his house. Max judged from the height of the headlights that it must be Betty's van. It passed the parlor's parking lot and climbed the road up the hill.

He glanced at Norma. "If you can finish this job alone, I'll go home."

She squeezed his arm. "Get on up there right now and talk to Betty. Don't let Audubon meddle in your affairs. He just can't stand the notion that he's turning into a lonely old man while everybody else gets happy."

Max didn't agree with that assessment of Audubon's motives. Audubon was in no danger of being lonely or old any time soon. He was, however, determined to defend his pet causes at all costs, and to acquire the people he wanted to help him.

Max kissed Norma on the cheek, then left the veranda to stride up the drive to the house. He found Betty seated on the bed in the guest room. She was scratching Faux Paw on the stomach. She looked up and smiled.

Max halted in the door, studying the calm, pleasant scene in surprise. "Hi. You worked later than I expected."

"I was at Grace's shop. The house has a cute little upstairs apartment. She uses it for storage, but there's still plenty of room. It could be comfortable. She's willing to rent it to me in exchange for free meals at the restaurant. And—"

"I know that Audubon came to see you today."

Her smile faded. The guest room was lit only by an ancient floor lamp in one corner, which had given her emotions some camouflage. But now there was no hiding the strained expression on her face. Moving to the foot of the bed, Max saw the puffiness around her eyes. She'd been crying.

"Don't," she said raggedly when he reached a hand toward her. She turned her face away so that a sheet of black hair cascaded alongside it, shielding her expression.

Max stood there in miserable silence, his hand in midair. Finally he dropped it to his side. He went to a

chair in one corner and sat down. "Tell me what he said."

"That he's known you for almost twenty years and you've never stayed in one place more than three years."

"The marines made those decisions for me, babe."

"But you've always told Audubon that you liked it that way . . . you'd be bored if you settled down."

"I said a lot of things when I was younger."

"You said it during your last assignment, right before you retired. When you were working in the Middle East. You said that you're like a shark—you have to keep moving, or you'll die."

"Men say a lot of macho crap when they don't have anything better to discuss. Audubon works on the fringe of the military. He's even worked for the military as a consultant at times. That's how he and I have stayed in touch over the years. But he doesn't know me as well as he thinks."

"Neither do I." She raked her hands through her hair and laughed wearily. "Audubon told me a lot about your work as commander of an antiterrorist team."

"I've told you about it myself. I've never tried to hide the fact that I've killed people in the line of duty. Or that I've nearly been killed myself a few times."

"I know. I understand. But—" she gestured, searching for words—"I never realized how different your life used to be. Totally different from now. The intrigue, the danger, the excitement." She looked at him in tragic bewilderment. "How can you be happy here? Audubon says that you can't be. That you may be content for now, but it's just a matter of time—"

"Who are you going to believe—me or a stranger with ulterior motives?" Max rose to his feet, angry and hurt. "I find your distrust pretty damned hard to take."

"It's not distrust." She shook her head wretchedly while she scanned his face for answers. "I don't think you're trying to deceive me about the future. I think you're deceiving yourself. You refuse to plan for the

future because you don't want to lose your freedom of choice."

"Does anyone? Do you? How do you know what you'll want years from now?"

"I know that I'll want a family, and a permanent home, and a husband who looks forward to sharing the rest of his life with me. I know that I want to start building that here, soon."

Max began to pace, fury growing inside him like a dark menace. "A piece of paper that says we're married— is that all it would take to make you happy? All right, dammit, let's get one. Let's get married."

"Stop it." A cry of pain and anger tore from her throat. She buried her head in her hands. Faux Paw bounded off the bed, looking perturbed by the strange noise, and skulked from the room.

Max halted, staring at Betty's huddled, miserable form. His fingernails dug into his palms. He was so afraid of losing her that he reached blindly for ways to keep her, even if they were harsh. "I chased you, but in the end it was you who made the decision to come to my bed. I never made promises I couldn't keep."

"I never said that you did." Her voice was distraught, but she laughed brokenly. Her laughter died quickly. "But I won't be a fool again." She raised her head and looked at him grimly. "I have to back away from this relationship before it ruins us both. I thought I could deal with it. But I can't. I love you too much."

"You're not backing away from it. That's impossible to do, and you know it."

"Watch me. I'm moving to town—"

"The hell you are." He hated what he was about to do, but he was desperate. "We're partners. Whether you want it that way or not."

Her eyes widened. "What do you mean?"

"I mean if you move out of this house, I'll sell your barbecue sauce recipe lock, stock, and mushrooms to the head honcho down at Goody Foods."

She covered her mouth and looked at him in horrified disbelief. "You couldn't know what's in that recipe."

Max walked to the chair and sat down on the edge of its seat. Leaning forward, he fixed a narrowed, unyielding gaze on her. "My grandfather was a sailor. He must have learned how to make the key ingredient somewhere in the Orient. He brought home an unusual variety of mushrooms. He grew them in the cellar. His notes say that after they're harvested, the secret is to put them in a keg of water and let them ferment. Then use the juice to make a sort of soy sauce, which is used as flavoriong in the barbecue sauce."

He could tell from her stricken expression that he had confirmed the truth. He didn't feel good about the aura of defeat in her eyes. "I could list the rest of the ingredients, if you want," he told her gruffly. "But they're pretty ordinary. Honey, ketchup, a few herbs—"

"All right. Now what?" She shut her eyes, took a deep breath, then watched him with troubled resolve. "You won't sell the recipe."

"How do you know that?"

"Because I know you. You're not capable of hurting me that way."

He bowed his head, fighting shame, but also proud that she trusted him. Her trust, however, could undermine his position. "I don't want to sabotage your business." He arched a brow. "All I want is an ironclad hold on your life."

"I see."

"We're going to be partners," he repeated. "I've got twenty-five thousand dollars stashed away. I'll be fair. What percentage of the business will you sell for that amount?"

"I don't want a partner who believes in blackmail."

"Look, babe, I know you don't *need* the money. But you don't have any choice."

"Are there any other stipulations?"

"You keep living here."

"No."

"You can have the guest room." He nearly strangled on those words.

She looked stunned. "It'll be awful this way, Max."

"Anything's better than having you move out."

"It won't work, Max. It won't solve our problem."

"I'll take my chances." He stood up and walked over to her. He held out his hand. "Deal?"

Tears slid down her face. A muscle worked in her throat. She shook his hand. "Deal. Fifty-fifty."

"That's more than fair."

"It's the only bargain you'll get from me."

He looked at her without victory. "I'll miss you tonight." He couldn't say anything else—his throat was raw and tight. He left the room and shut the door gently.

Ten

"Your mother likes me."

He made that announcement the next night as he passed her in the hall. It had been a horrible day, from the strained, silent breakfast with him, through the lunch at the restaurant, when he'd stopped in to casually hand her a check for $25,000, to this evening. They'd spent the past several hours avoiding each other.

Betty halted and looked up at him. She tried to ignore the fact that he was wearing nothing but a white robe open halfway to his navel. She pulled her own robe tighter around her pajamas. "You spoke to my mother? When?"

"When you were in the shower. She called. She invited me to the party this weekend. I confessed that you hadn't mentioned it to me."

"I wasn't planning to go."

"You are now. I told her so."

"It's one of those formal things, Max. Mother and Father host it every year around Thanksgiving. Surely you don't want to spend an evening trussed up in a rented tuxedo."

"No. But since I own a very comfortable tuxedo—two of them, in fact—I won't mind."

She cast her eyes down and mumbled, "I suppose I was judging a book by its camouflage again."

He accepted her apology with a gracious nod. "By the way. Your mother is charming. A little flaky, but I mean that as a compliment. It was like talking to a hummingbird."

"Be glad she's a progressive hummingbird. I don't know how to even begin to explain the living arrangement here, and I hope she and Pop don't ask."

"Oh, I explained. I said that we love each other and are living in sin, although we're taking a temporary break from the sin part." When she looked at him askance, he chuckled wickedly. "I said that you were a guest here. That's all I said."

"That's all I am." She started past. "We'll promenade to my nouveau riche ancestral home, if you insist. I'll borrow a dress—"

"Whoa." He took her arm. Even through her robe and pajamas, the contact sent rivers of sensation along her skin and deep into her most defenseless desires. He stepped closer, his gaze on her mouth. "You'll *borrow* a dress? Why?"

"There are little piles of ashes where my formal dresses used to hang."

"Why not buy a few new ones? I thought you were the woman who could wreak destruction in Neiman-Marcus with a sharp charge card."

She clasped her chest melodramatically. "What, buy my formal gowns off the rack? How tacky."

"Betty, is there something about your finances—"

"We're business partners. The business finances are your only concern. You saw the records at lunch. They're fine."

"And your personal finances?"

"Are personal." She tried to draw her arm away. He held it long enough to keep her still for his kiss. It was a light, tender caress that left her shivering and upset. "Good night, Max," she said tearfully.

"Good night." He didn't look any better than she felt.

• • •

Max handed the Jeep's keys to a valet and went to the passenger side. Ordinarily he would have been inclined to turn his attention to the magnificent antebellum home that loomed in front of him, or to study the massive oaks and perfect gardens.

But it was impossible to stop looking at Betty. She took his hand and descended from the Jeep regally. Her gown shimmered like liquid gold. It draped from her shoulders, baring the smooth white beauty of her neck and back. The sleeves tapered to slender tubes at her wrists, emphasizing the grace of her hands. The skirt hugged her with enough decorum for a mother and father's approval, but the slit up one side revealed her leg in a way that won a very different kind of approval from Max.

Small clusters of diamonds decorated her earlobes, and a matching pendant lay delicately on her chest, drawing the eye immediately to the gown's neckline and the slightest, most tantalizing hint of cleavage there.

He enjoyed looking at her so much that he didn't even mind looking at Faux Paw too. Betty tugged on her leash and called softly. The cat clambered from behind the passenger seat and jumped to the driveway.

"My Jeep has never been so honored," Max told her as he closed the passenger door behind her. "I should make a picture of you and the party animal standing next to it."

"Flattery."

"No. You look incredible, babe."

Her cheeks flushed at the compliment, though she regarded him with carefully shuttered eyes. The past few days had been pure hell for both him and her. Hopefully, tonight would be a reprieve from the tension. He begged silently for there to be a dance orchestra, so that he would have an excuse to hold her.

Perhaps they could make sense out of the torment they were causing each other.

He corrected himself grimly. The torment that he was causing her. The torment that he questioned more each day.

They walked under a marble portico to a massive entranceway flanked by butlers. Faux Paw prowled beside Betty, straining at the leash and hissing in the butler's direction. Max laughed wearily. "I feel like a tour guide at a formal zoo."

"You sound so tired. Are you all right?"

"After hardly sleeping for the past few nights? Hell, no," he whispered back. "Are you?"

She smiled a little. "Hell, no."

"You haven't complimented me on my good looks. I'm depressed, that's all."

"I thought I gave you a clue when you came into the living room tonight. Didn't all the staring and the stammering tell you something?"

"I thought you were just overcome by my cologne."

She laughed for the first time in days. "You look magnificent in a tux, Major."

He held out his arm and she slipped her hand around the elbow. They shared a private look before the butlers opened the stately old doors for them. In it she communicated both sorrow and affection. They were a team, no matter what, with bonds that couldn't be destroyed. Would never be destroyed, he realized.

His chest swelled with pride for her, with pride at belonging to her. *But you don't belong to her*, he reminded himself. Not in a way that the world would recognize, at least. Not in a way that said he was sworn to her for life, that she was sworn to him.

He wondered if all he needed was one small leap of faith. He began to pray that he could make it.

Her father had kidnapped Max for interrogation. They were smoking cigars together in the library, and she

didn't doubt that her father was trying to determine whether Max had money or at least the ambition to make money. Those were the criteria by which her father judged most men. Poor Sloan, with his bohemian attitude toward high finance, had infuriated her father. She doubted that her father would ever forgive her for spending her money on Sloan's career. She had stopped expecting him to understand, and she made certain that she never asked for his help, financial or otherwise. His help was attached to criticism.

Sloan had a lucrative recording contract now and was rolling in money. Betty shrugged. She didn't miss Sloan, but the irony was bitter. Pensively her thoughts turned to Max. He had no ulterior motives for needing her. He wasn't Sloan. He was a different threat altogether, and one that she didn't really expect to escape. She hardly knew whether she wanted to escape.

She sipped champagne in a quiet corner and searched the enormous crowd that filled the ballroom. She spied her mother, fluttering about in a ruffled black gown. Max had been correct about her. She looked like a hummingbird as she flitted from one elite guest to the next, sipping the honey from their admiration.

She was a loving mother, a sweet mother. But she was, and had always been, a totally self-centered mother, with not the slightest comprehension of anyone's problems but her own. Betty had learned long ago to take care of herself.

And then there was her father. Smart, tough, blustery. Having dragged himself up the social and economic ladder, he now enjoyed perching at the top and looking down smugly. He was determined that no one would accuse his child of having less gumption than he'd had. *Fat little rich girl.* How many times had he called her that, claiming that humiliation provoked determination?

Betty swallowed the last of her champagne and nod-

ded wryly to herself. Well, he'd been right. She was determined to get everything she wanted from life. She was determined never to be humiliated again, by anyone. She was so determined that she was letting pride strangle her most precious relationship. She shut her eyes, thinking of Max.

"Beebee. My God, look at you."

The familiar male voice shocked her. She swung about and faced its owner. His tux was loosely cut in a nonchalant style more at home on the West Coast; his tie was his favorite color, a deep chartreuse; he wore his usual ruby stud earring, shaped like a guitar. Sloan Richards had always been colorful.

And handsome. Under a mop of winsome auburn hair he smiled at her, dimples crinkling around his mouth, boyish blue eyes lighting happily. She should have been breathless and charmed. Not so many months ago, she would have been.

"You're a party crasher," she said calmly. "I certainly didn't ask my folks to invite you."

His smile faded. He was great at looking hurt—puppyish and solemn, as if he'd just been spanked for chewing a shoe. "I flew in from the Coast to see you," he said softly. "I knew this annual hoedown would be my best chance." There was enormous sincerity in his eyes, which didn't surprise her. But the anguish in them did.

She stood on tiptoe and kissed his cheek. He hugged her. They stepped apart and stood looking at each other in leaden silence. She couldn't think of much to say to him. How had she ever thought that their long conversations about him, his music, and his dreams were fascinating?

"Things are going well, I assume?" she asked politely.

"Yes. No. The album's coming along great. But I miss you. Can we go somewhere and talk?"

She nodded. They walked down a hallway done in ostentatious French antiques. Louis the something-or-

other. She could never remember which Louis her mother favored.

Sloan reached for her hands. She resolutely clasped them behind her back. His expression grew more troubled. "I want to make things up to you, Beebee."

"There's nothing to make up. We said our good-byes."

"But I was rotten to you."

"Yes, you were."

"After all those years of waiting for me to grow up, after all the good times and the love, and all the money you spent to help me—"

"Gratitude and apologies accepted. Are you trying to ask me for more help? If you recall, I'm broke. And a lot wiser."

"And I'm rich. And a lot wiser." He rested his hands on her arms and looked down at her with a yearning expression. "I'm not here to ask you for help. I'm here to see if we can start over. I want you to come out to L.A. with me, Beebee."

"You asked me to do that before."

"In a pretty arrogant way, as I recall. Something like, 'Be my main groupie, would you?' "

"Those were pretty much the words you used."

"Beebee, I've seen the light. It's a cold, lonely world out there. It's crazy. I need some stability in my life." He took a deep breath. "I need someone to be there for me. Someone who's always going to be there. You."

"I was there for years. You kept looking over my head."

He squeezed her shoulders. "Not anymore. I'm looking straight at you, Beebee. And I'm asking you to marry me."

Betty was stunned. Not pleased, she realized immediately, just amazed that after being apart for almost a year, without even a phone call between them, he had waltzed into this party and asked her to marry him.

"I waited five years for that proposal," she reminded him. "Its's a little late now."

"Oh, I know you need time to regroup. I'm going to be here for a week. Why don't you and I duck out of this party and go to my hotel—"

"Excuse me," another masculine voice interjected. "But I could swear that you're making a pass at my lady."

Betty gasped softly. She had forgotten how silently Max could walk. Not that she had anything to hide. He lounged against a wall several yards away, his arms crossed over his chest, one foot propped over the other, the picture of relaxation. The slit-eyed appraisal he gave Sloan was the only indication of his mood.

Sloan shot a startled look from Max to her. "Really, Beebee?"

"Really."

"Is he important to you?"

"Yes."

"More important than I used to be?"

"I don't really owe you any information about my life."

Sloan frowned. "I can deal with competition."

"You're not even in the game anymore."

Max sauntered up and stood to one side, smiling without a trace of warmth. "You must be Sloan Richards."

Betty hurriedly introduced them. She had never seen Sloan look jealous before. She had never given him any reason to.

He chewed his lower lip and scowled. "Beebee, I know I have a lot to make up for," he said slowly. "I still love you, Beebee. I want to marry you. In a church, with flowers, cake, a honeymoon, the whole thing. I want us to have kids together. I want you to be a success with your work. You can start a great barbecue restaurant in L.A. I'll help you."

Betty shook her head. She could feel Max watching her. Why couldn't he be the one making this kind of impassioned offer? Hearing it from Sloan was like a cruel joke. "I'll call you," she told Sloan numbly.

"We'll meet for lunch. This isn't the time or place to—"

"Good night, Mr. Richards." Max took her arm. He didn't put any pressure on it, but he held it firmly.

Sloan shook his head doggedly. There was an aura of wounded loneliness about him. Betty reached out impulsively and touched his arm. "We'll talk later. Where are you staying?"

"At the Ritz-Carlton." He gestured numbly toward Max. "Beebee, you're not seriously involved with this straight-edged character, are you? You're not engaged or anything, right?"

"I'm not engaged," she said grimly. "You'd better stop talking while you're ahead."

Max chuckled coolly. "Take her advice, Mr. Richards."

Sloan pointed at Max but looked at Betty. "He's so old, Beebee."

"Old?" Max gave him a warning look, but smiled sardonically. "I'll be thirty-nine in April. Why, if my pacemaker weren't on the blink, I'd let myself get upset. How many years have *you* been shaving?"

Betty felt a headache coming on. She looked up at Max sheepishly. "Sloan is twenty-six."

Max stared at her for a second. "Cradle robber."

Sloan groaned dramatically. "Beebee, you have to give me a chance."

She bristled. "All those years, I thought I was waiting for you to catch up with my maturity. But now it occurs to me that I'm not that much older than you. You should have caught up a long time ago."

"I've caught up now." He grabbed one of her hands and kissed it. "We'll have lunch, just like you said. Okay?"

"Lunch. All right."

"Lunch, no," Max interjected. "It's a waste of time."

Sloan shot him a curt glance. "Don't count your chickens before they hatch, grandpa."

"Watch it. I'll hit you with my cane."

"Good night, Sloan," Betty said quickly.

But Sloan was relentless. "Beebee, listen. I know I made mistakes. I used your money. Hell, I practically bankrupted you. But you knew it was for a good cause. And look at me now"—he held out his arms—"I'm a success because you loved and supported a struggling, idealistic musician. Let me make it up to you."

Her humiliation was terrible. Max knew her financial secret, that she had been a fool, that she was struggling now because of it, that she needed his help more than she'd ever wanted him to know. His fingers dug into her arm, and she looked at him with defensive dignity.

His face was a mask of anger. "I think you and I need to talk without the wonder boy present."

"Yes." She shook her head at Sloan.

"Call me, Beebee—"

"Good night," Max said in a low voice full of warning.

Betty let him lead her down the hall. His stride was long and quick, his hand a vise on her arm. "There," she told him grimly, pointing toward a side hall. "Let's go to the garden room."

When they reached an artistically lighted atrium filled with potted trees and plants, he faced her, a muscle popping in his jaw, the green ice of his eyes chilling her. "Why didn't you tell me that you were broke?"

"I didn't want to explain the reason."

"Is this your idea of how to treat someone you love—by keeping secrets?"

"My mistakes are private. I handle them myself."

"That's a strange attitude for a woman who claims to live and breathe for the spirit of marriage, the sharing, commitment, and trust."

"You don't want to be a marriage candidate. Why should you care if I don't treat you like one?"

"But you considered that overage teenager a good prospect?"

"I made a mistake," she said between gritted teeth. "I resolved it."

"Not if you're planning to have lunch with it."

"Lunch does not mean romantic involvement."

"I'm asking you not to see him again."

"You don't have that right."

They traded a look of troubled challenge. She was miserable with Max's jealousy; there was no satisfaction in hurting him over Sloan's reappearance. Max stiffened with pride. "I didn't think you'd stoop to playing me against another man, but that's what it feels like at the moment."

She took a faltering step back from him, so shocked that she almost stumbled. "You think I'd try to pressure you into marrying me?" She clenched her fists. "Relax, Major. I have too much self-esteem to play that game. I want a man to propose of his own free will."

"Well, Sloan's probably still waiting in the hall."

His words whipped her. She told herself that he didn't mean them, but the pain went too deep. "I hope so," she retorted softly. "I'd like to talk to him."

"I'm leaving. Stop this grandstanding and come with me."

"Or else?"

He smiled thinly. "Or else I'm leaving alone."

"What? No threats about selling my sauce recipe to Goody Foods? No threats about taking back your investment? No threats about our future relationship—excuse me, I forgot." She gave a choking laugh. "You don't believe in thinking about the future." She pressed trembling fingertips to the corners of her eyes, willing the tears back. "Go ahead, Max. Make some threats."

He looked at her wretchedly. "Not my style, babe. You'd know that I didn't mean them, anyway. Now come on. Let's go home."

His honest anguish nearly crumpled her. "Max, go without me," she urged in a tortured voice. "Don't you understand? It's not my home; it's yours."

"I can't believe that you look at the situation that way."

"I do. I'm so afraid that I'll stay with you, and then one day I'll lose you. And I wouldn't be fit for any other man afterward, because nobody could take your place."

"I'm hurting you," he said hoarsely. "And not accomplishing anything. I want us to be together all the time, and I want to share everything in your life. Can't we find any middle ground?"

"We did, for a little while. And it was so wonderful that I can't risk it anymore." She hugged herself tightly, feeling as if she were about to fall apart. "Go. Please go. This has nothing to do with Sloan showing up here tonight. You and I were headed for this moment all along."

They were silent, the seconds passing in mute despair. Finally, like a man coming out of a trance, he shook his head. "I'll be waiting. The front door will be unlocked."

Betty turned away blindly and steeled herself from the urge to give up all her convictions and follow him. "I'll be staying with my parents for the next day or two."

He came up close behind her and rested both hands on her shoulders. "This isn't over, babe."

Betty quivered as he kissed her hair gently. She listened to the sound of his footsteps on the room's tile floor as he left. Slow, subdued, but firm. He always meant what he said.

Max slumped on the edge of the couch, smoothing a scarf of Betty's between his hands. She would have to come back, if only to get her clothes. It had only been two days. Slowly he raised his gaze to a dark window beside the fireplace. His eyes were raw from lack of sleep, and his head throbbed.

Cold rain drizzled down the windowpanes. He smiled sarcastically at the drama of the scene—the bleak night, the empty house, his angry, self-questioning mood.

Ah, yes, it was good to be independent and live only for the moment. It felt wonderful.

He stared at the phone on the coffee table. It compelled him to curse softly and viciously. He had waited for two days. Now, without pride, he grabbed the phone receiver and punched the number for Betty's parents' home.

Her mother answered. Max made a gallant attempt to chat with her nonchalantly before he asked to speak with Betty. In a breathless, honeyed voice, Emily Quint explained that Betty had gone to Los Angeles for the week with a friend.

He didn't fluster her further by asking who the friend was. He knew. She knew that he knew. He thanked her and hung up. Then he leaned back on the couch and closed his eyes. The scarf felt like a whisper of good-bye in his hands.

The sunset was a smoggy red glow over Los Angeles. "To think that this view belongs to me!" Sloan exclaimed. Standing on the deck of his little Spanish-style house, he spread his arms and surveyed the city below them. "Do you know how much I had to pay for a view like this?"

Betty settled in a patio chair and set her soft drink on a glass-topped table beside it. "Too much."

He laughed. "Right. But it's worth it." He ambled to the table, shoving his hands into the pockets of white trousers. With the trousers he wore an unstructured pink jacket with the sleeves pushed up to his elbows. The pink T-shirt underneath his jacket bore the name of his band, Play by Heart.

"So what do you want to do tonight, Beebee? Breeze through a few more clubs? How about dinner at Spago's again?" He rocked back and forth on the heels of his white loafers. "Or how about we just stay here and move your luggage from the guest bedroom to the master bedroom? Hmmm?"

She laughed. "No thanks. I like the guest bedroom."

"Beebee, what's the point?" Frowning, he sat down across the table from her and propped his chin on his hands. "We've done the 'pals' thing for three days now. We've gotten reacquainted. When do we get back to basics?"

"I never said that we were going to. I only said that I wanted to observe you in your natural habitat. And that I wanted us to be friends again."

"But I thought—"

"I wanted to teach myself a lesson, Sparky."

"Sparky. That's the first time you've used my nickname. I love it."

"You'll always be Sparky to me. Even when you're a superstar, and you're on the cover of *Rolling Stone*, and women are throwing themselves in front of your limousine, I'll still think of you as Sparky."

"I don't like the implications here. What did you mean about teaching yourself a lesson?"

"You and I had some great times together. I can remember them without feeling angry at you now. I'm learning to enjoy one day at a time, Sparky."

"But don't forget to think about the future. Marriage. Children." He spread his arms grandly. "I'm ready."

"Good. I wish you luck finding the right woman." She smiled pensively at him. "I have to go home and make some sense of my life."

He deflated like a handsome pink balloon. "I sort of expected this," he said glumly. "You're going back to the old marine."

"I'm going back to be *near* him, yes. Because I feel good about the future, and I have to believe that I can make him feel the same way." She went to Sloan and kissed him on the forehead. "Thank you for confirming that I did some things right in the past."

"You were the best. You're still the best." He looked up at her with tears in his eyes. "Beebee, will you let me give you some money? I owe you so much."

She chucked him under the chin. "Don't spoil a gift that was given in love. I really don't regret anything I did for you."

He smiled sadly. "But I get the feeling that I was just the warm-up before the real concert. You and Dudley Dooright."

"I don't know if Dudley will *ever* do right, but I think I'll fly home tomorrow and see him."

"I'm gonna dedicate the album to you."

She was so pleased that she choked up. Sloan stood. They hugged each other tightly. "Sparky?"

"Hmmm?"

"Just don't use my initials."

Max's schedule of cases was light for the day, and he finished an hour early. He left the courthouse and drove home slowly, his thoughts lethargic. Rain slashed down on the windshield. Through an exhausting output of willpower, he kept himself from thinking about Betty. So she was with Sloan, in sunny L.A. But she was *not* in Sloan's bed.

Max believed that without doubt. It wasn't her way. He had faith. For the first time in years faith was sweeping through him like a desperately welcome breeze in a desert.

But still, thinking about her, knowing that she wasn't going to share his nights and his days anymore, at least not any time soon, was torture. He made himself think about the three weddings he was scheduled to perform that evening. All were costume packages.

The marriage parlor was losing its appeal. He didn't find it funny to preside over one wedding after another, when each reminded him of the problem between him and Betty. He didn't like watching the couples and wondering, as he'd never wondered before, if they were destined for much fuller, happier lives than he was.

Muttering darkly to his self-doubts, he parked the

Jeep behind the house because the back door was quicker to reach. He bolted inside and went straight to his bedroom. Damp, exhausted, and depressed, he stretched out on the futon without undressing, and fell asleep.

He awoke to a deafening explosion and the roar of flames.

Eleven

It had been raining when her jet landed at the airport, but now a sapphire sky emerged from the clouds. The sun sparkled coldly on the windshield of the Mercedes she'd borrowed from her mother. Her mother had jokingly threatened to tie Faux Paw to the back bumper. Clumsy Faux Paw had not been the ideal houseguest in a house filled with expensive knickknacks.

Faux Paw would be coming back to Webster Springs as soon as Betty arranged the apartment over Grace's shop. Troubled, Betty turned up the car's heater and shivered inside a heavy green sweater she'd pulled over her shirtwaist dress. She hadn't prepared for the change from Los Angeles to north Georgia temperatures. But she also shivered from anticipation.

She was going to be the woman who changed Maximilian Templeton's opinion of marriage and family life. It might take a while, but she'd do it. Such faith would have struck her as foolish a few days ago, but Sloan had given her back her pride. Believing in Sloan hadn't been a mistake, even though marrying him would have been a big one.

Now she had the confidence to accept whatever happened between her and Max. She was going to show

him that his dark distrust of the future was no match for her patience, dignity, and love.

Forested hills swept past her as the road climbed toward Webster Springs. She sighed with relief. Home. Max. The two were the same.

He should be finished with his work at the courthouse by this time of day. She'd stop by his house and see him. They'd talk. She'd explain about Sloan and the trip to L.A. She'd explain that she wasn't going to brood about the past if Max would stop brooding about the future.

Maybe Max would go into town with her and help get the apartment ready. Later, maybe they'd celebrate this new phase of their relationship with some barbecue and a bottle of muscadine wine. She smiled, thinking of other ways to celebrate.

Her smile froze in horror as soon as she turned into the drive below Max's place. Up on the hill a charred, smoldering shell was all that remained of his house. The apple trees in the front yard were scorched. The remnant of the flag pole was a thin black spindle. The lawn was a muddy mess cut by the tracks of fire engines. Ruined furniture was scattered everywhere.

She was dimly aware of screaming Max's name as she slammed the Mercedes into the graveled lot by the wedding parlor. She threw herself from the car and ran to find Norma. The parlor had a cold, deserted look. The unlit "Get Hitched" sign stared down at her cheerlessly.

Betty pounded on the front door. Norma must be wherever Max was. The hospital? The *morgue*?

Gulping for air, Betty raced back to the car. She did her best to drive slowly and safely into town, but by the time she reached the square, she had run off the edge of the road twice and clipped the passenger-side mirror on a mailbox. She didn't dare take her eyes off the road long enough to look at the speedometer.

A patrol car from the sheriff's department swung out of a side street and followed her, lights flashing, to the

small hospital on a hill east of town. Betty parked the Mercedes with one wheel atop the curb at the emergency-room entrance. She bolted for the doors, while a deputy trotted after her, calling firmly for her to stop.

She ran inside and nearly collided with paramedics covered in mud and soot. Betty took a quick, terrified look at them and staggered to the admissions window. "Max Templeton!" she said to the startled young woman behind the window. "Is he here?"

"Ma'am, you're in trouble," the deputy said, arriving behind her and grabbing her arm.

Betty hung on to the ledge of the admissions window. "Is Max Templeton here?"

The clerk blinked anxiously. "Y-yes, ma'am."

"Oh, my God." Betty pivoted blindly and stared at the doors to the treatment areas. "Max!"

The paramedics gave her curious looks and stepped closer. The deputy clung to her arm. He said something authoritative, but it was a meaningless buzz in her ears. She lurched forward, twisted away from him, and gave him a shove. Caught off guard, he stumbled into the paramedics. All three men bumped into a watercooler, and it fell over with a boom that reverberated down the corridor.

Betty ran for the doors to the treatment area. She plowed through them and met a bewildering array of emergency-room equipment and personnel. A nurse started toward her, shaking her head. "This area is off-limits, ma'am—"

"I'm here to see Max Templeton!"

"You'll have to wait outside, ma'am."

Betty dodged her. She scrambled through an obstacle course of gurneys, scanning a distant corner where individual screens hid other gurneys. She heard shouts and running feet behind her.

They had hidden him. He must be dead. Fear numbed her as she ran from one screen to the next. The gurneys behind the first three were empty. A deputy grabbed

her. She elbowed him in the ribs and their combined momentum carried them past the last screen.

Betty slammed into the wall. Gasping, she looked fearfully at the last gurney. A groan of relief burst from her throat. "Max!"

He looked terrible—bruised, muddy, his face covered in grime and his clothes a damp mess. He was propped up on pillows. A bloody cocoon of gauze surrounded his left hand. He stared at her in groggy amazement as she careened to his side.

"What happened? Are you all right?" Her hands flew over him, patting his chest and stomach. "My God, Max. Max, are you okay?"

"He's fine," a deputy grumbled. "But you're under arrest."

Max finally dragged his eyes from her to the small army of deputies, paramedics, and nurses behind her. He shook his head at them. "She's not always like this. Sometimes she's worse."

Betty weakly bowed her head to his shoulder and held his good hand. "I thought you were . . . but you're not. You're not."

The deputy cleared his throat. "Does, uhmmm, this lady belong to you, Judge?"

"Yes," Betty answered. "Whether he wants me or not."

She felt Max's fingers tightening around her hand. "She's with me. I'll take responsibility if she goes berserk again."

Betty looked toward the group. "I apologize," she said in a voice that shook. "I just . . . I didn't know anything except that the house"—she swiveled her attention to Max—"your house!"

"You and I don't have much luck with home ownership, do we?" He winced as he shifted his injured hand. His tired, bloodshot eyes caressed her face. He was silent, studying her with a heart-wrenching welcome, a look that made her lean closer to him and stroke his cheek tenderly.

The others left, whispering among themselves. Betty

sat down limply by Max's side. Her throat wouldn't let words pass. She shook her head in bittersweet frustration. "What happened?"

"Our cellar rat wanted revenge."

She covered her throat. "The man we caught in my basement? From the robbery?"

Max nodded with painful effort. "He made bail while he was waiting for his trial. I don't know if he had anything to do with the fire at your place, but he definitely paid a visit to mine. He rigged a gas line."

She felt sick. "He was trying to kill you?"

"Honestly, no. The stupid bastard was just trying to burn my house down. He didn't know I was in it." Max shut his eyes and smiled thinly. "Now he knows."

"You caught him yourself?"

"When the explosion happened I was asleep in the bedroom. The house nearly caved in. I woke up with the bedroom full of smoke and the floor half gone. I crawled to a window and broke the glass with my hand. I saw our friend heading for the woods behind the house. I went after him."

She made a keening sound and looked at the bloody gauze. "How bad are you hurt?"

"I'll need a few dozen stitches. Nothing serious."

"Oh. Nothing *serious*," she repeated numbly. "Did you . . . Where is that guy? Can I see him? Can I take a baseball bat with me when I do?"

"Too late. He's upstairs. In surgery. Having his jaw wired and his nose fixed." Max's expression was troubled. "There was a moment when I wanted to kill him. I could have done it easily."

"But you didn't."

He managed a hint of the cocky smile she knew so well. It was terribly sad. "I'm getting soft and sentimental."

She smothered a sob and kissed him. "You're not soft. And I like you sentimental."

In a hoarse voice he whispered, "Good. I need a hug damned fast."

She cried out and carefully put her arms around

him. Betty nestled her head against his shoulder. "I suppose the house is a total loss. Did the firemen save anything?"

"No." His voice was leaden. "Including what was left of your clothes."

"Maximilian, are we under some sort of curse, or what?"

"Looks that way." But his good hand was stroking her hair in a way that said he wasn't thinking about their bad luck at the moment. "But you came back."

"I live here, you know."

A long breath shuddered from his chest. "For good?"

"For good. I just went out to California to get my priorities straight." She knotted her fingers in his damp, dirty shirt. "That's *all* I did. Do you savvy, Major?"

"I savvy," he whispered.

"Where's Norma?"

"I asked her to go buy me something clean to wear."

The enormity of his loss began to sink in. She cried softly and held him tighter. "I'm so sorry, love."

"Now we're both homeless and clothesless. I'm even Jeep-less, because the damned thing was sitting right next to the house."

"Please tell me that you have insurance."

"The Jeep is covered. The house, well, sort of."

"Max!"

"My father only had it insured for twenty thousand. I hadn't gotten around to changing the policy. Do you know what twenty thousand dollars will build in to-day's market?"

"A nice two-seater outhouse?"

"Right."

They were both silent. "So we're in the same boat," she said finally.

"And it seems to be sinking, fast. A helluva mess."

She felt a sharp pang of disappointment. Couldn't he even consider the possibility of them building a new home and a new life together? Betty bit her tongue and

silently swore to love him as he was and hope for the best.

She sat up and gently began straightening his hair with her fingertips. "Let's live for the moment, Major."

He looked at her with dull surprise. "I don't believe you said that."

"We'll get your hand stitched up, then we'll move our tired fannies to a quiet, comfortable room over at the new inn that opened last week."

"Betty—"

"I've heard that the rooms have hot tubs."

He wound his good hand under her hair and cupped the back of her head, holding her still as he scrutinized her. Betty caught her breath. "What's wrong, Max?"

"Nothing," he said finally. "I'm not going to question this too much. I'm just so damned glad you're back. I love you. All I want is to be alone with you and not think about anything beyond today."

She nodded, hiding her sorrow.

He was in pain, and the least of it was physical. Max was no more than vaguely aware of his bruises, aching muscles, and injured hand. He pulled Betty closer to him, spoon style, and watched her sleep. The soft light of a lamp beside the inn's antique bedstead gleamed on her black hair and cast a golden tone on her skin. She had never looked more beautiful.

Bittersweet anger tore at him. He had so little to offer her now. How would it sound if he suddenly asked her to spend the rest of her life with him? Manipulative, that's how—as if he had nothing else to lose and was making a commitment out of desperation.

No, that was no way to convince her that this tiger was changing his stripes. He needed to approach her from a position of power, of money, so that she'd know that he was sincere.

His eyes narrowed in thought as he glanced at the nightstand. His wallet lay there. It was the only per-

sonal possession he'd been able to save. Inside it was Audubon's card. Max grimaced. Fate had an interesting way of narrowing life's choices.

Betty stirred sleepily, twisted inside the circle of his arms, and nuzzled her face against his chest. She stretched, giving him a naked full-body caress that made him catch his breath. She seemed to sense that he was watching her. She tilted her head back and looked straight into his eyes, frowning benignly. "You okay?"

"Yes. Enjoying the view," he assured her.

Her worried scrutiny told him that she wasn't satisfied with that answer. All evening she had fussed over him, brushing his hair while he soaked in the hot tub that graced one corner of the room, slipping bite-sized chunks of pizza into his mouth as he lounged in bed, giving him a rubdown with a hot, soothing liniment, then giving him the sweetest kind of soothing with her mouth.

Now she rolled onto her back but remained snuggled against him. Slowly she drew her fingertips to his face and traced the lines of fatigue around his eyes. "Don't think about what happened today," she urged gently. "Everything will be okay. Try to sleep."

He kissed the tip of her nose. "I'm fine, babe. I'm just trying to decide how to reciprocate all the TLC you've given me tonight."

"I'll take an IOU for the TLC."

"Gee! Keep it on the QT, BBQ, but you're OK."

They both began to chuckle. In the midst of it he realized how extraordinary it was that she could make him laugh after such a rotten day. He reached under the covers, stroking her from breasts to thighs with slow, loving care. "Here's my RSVP."

She feigned surprise. "I wasn't aware that I'd issued an invitation."

"You can't see the glow in your eyes. It's definitely an invitation." With gentle exploration he found where

she was warmest and softest. "You should see your eyes now," Max told her gruffly.

She quivered, arching against his hand. Her expression was suffused with a devotion that humbled him. Her lips moved almost soundlessly. *Make love to me.*

His mouth touched hers, absorbing the words, and returning them. Tomorrow would arrive too soon. He prayed that she'd understand.

It was ridiculous to be this happy. She had no house, no furniture, and no more clothes than had been in a suitcase in the trunk of her mother's car.

Betty sipped her orange juice and smiled at Max over breakfast. Sunshine filtered through the restaurant's lace curtains; the dining room was warm with contentment. It would be an hour or more before Andy arrived for the day. Right now she and Max were the only ones in the house. They'd scrambled eggs and made pancakes in the big commercial kitchen, hardly a place she would have called romantic, but lovely when viewed through the afterglow of a tender, caring night.

He smiled back, though his face was lined with fatigue. His left hand was heavily bandaged; he gingerly rested it on the table. His eyes were shadowed by dark thoughts. He engaged in a one-handed battle with his pancakes. His weapons were a knife and a pat of butter.

"Would you like me to help?" she asked. "I could cut the pancakes up into small pieces for you."

He chuckled dryly. "No way. Aunt Jemima and I refuse to wimp out."

She looked at him pensively. "Your self-sufficiency is duly noted."

"I may be down, but I'm not out." His tone was sardonic. He jabbed his knife into the pancakes. "Care to hear any other clichés?"

Betty slowly set her glass of juice down. "Max, I want you to take back your investment in the barbecue sauce. We'll work something else out. We'll still be partners—"

"No. I'm not helpless. You need that money for the business. I intend to carry my weight. You went through enough money problems with Sloan Richards. I don't want to be compared to him."

"It's not even remotely the same situation," she said with growing alarm. "Max, what's the real issue here? Why are you talking like this?"

"I'm trying to do what's best for you. Because I love you."

His scowl sent a chill through her serenity. "You know, if two people love each other, sometimes one of them lets the other one carry the weight. They know that there's nothing humiliating about it." She fumbled with her napkin and carefully folded it into pleats. "It's not as if I'm trying to hog-tie you with a set of purse strings."

He tossed his knife down and pushed himself back from the table. He leveled a hard gaze at her. "I didn't say that you were trying to manipulate me."

"But you seem to be dead set against accepting more of my help." Her heart was trapped in her throat. "Feeling a little too dependent on me after yesterday? I thought you enjoyed being loved and cared for. Was I wrong? Are you determined to make certain that I don't get my hopes up about our future together?"

"We're getting away from the subject. I'm talking about money."

Dread stilled her. She hardly breathed. "No," she whispered. "It's something else. Why don't you just get it over with? Tell me what we're really talking about."

"When you were in the shower this morning, I placed a call to Audubon. He wasn't in, but he'll return the call eventually."

She clutched the edge of the table. "You're not going to . . . you wouldn't—"

"There's a helluva lot of money to be made working for Audubon. And it's not as if the work if selfish. Protecting people, getting them out of tight situations, perhaps even saving their lives—it's honorable. I wouldn't

feel that I was resigning as local magistrate without good reason."

"You need . . . the money more than the glory."

His expression hardened. He held her gaze with unblinking honesty. "Yes. But I'm not deserting you or this town. I'll be back. I plan to build a new home here—a damned nice home."

Trembling, she rose and planted her hands on the tabletop. Leaning toward him, her body rigid with control, she said softly, "I don't think you'll be back. I think this is an excuse to escape."

"No, babe." He stood also and grasped her by one arm. His anguished gaze told her he wasn't happy about the pain that he was causing her. "I know that you can't believe I'll be back—"

"How long would this exercise in pride take?"

"I don't know. It depends on the assignments that Audubon offers me. A few months, a year—"

"I won't see you at all during that time?"

"Of course you'll see me. I'll be here every chance I get."

"But Audubon gave me the impression that he's very demanding."

"He is. That's why he's worth working for. That's also why he makes his offers so lucrative."

"You'll be in some far corner of the world most of the time."

"Making the world a little better place, if I can," he replied dully.

"You've been doing a good job of that here. With people who respect you and need you. People like the little boy, Christopher, at Halloween. People like the elderly couple who had a wonderful wedding because of your generosity." *People like me*, she added silently. *Who will curl up and wither if you leave.*

"Think of it this way," he told her, his voice strained. "I'll have a lot of money to invest in our partnership."

Her shoulders slumped. What could she do—repeat what she feared was the truth—that he was looking for

an excuse to put distance between her and himself? He'd only deny it. It was obvious that he hated hurting her like this.

"When do you expect to hear from Audubon?" she asked with forced nonchalance.

"I don't know. I left the phone number for Norma's place, because that's where I'll be." He smiled thinly, his troubled gaze searching her face. "A minor delay interrupted my schedule yesterday. I have a backlog of weddings."

She stared at him miserably and said nothing. His hand tightened on her arm. "Come here, babe." But he was the one who moved, angling around the table and taking her deeply into his arms. She stood there in silent despair, clasping his waist with cold fingers, trying very hard to understand how love could mask such terrible surprises.

"It's not what you think," he whispered against her ear. "I love you. I'm not deserting you. Give me a chance to prove that."

"I don't have any choice."

He held her obstinately, his uninjured hand caressing the small of her back; she clenched her hands into fists against his sides but let her head rest on his shoulder. Anger, confusion, and love were struggling inside her; she didn't know which was dominant.

"We'll talk about this a lot more," he assured her in a gruff, unhappy voice.

"Later. Right now I . . . I have some thinking to do. And a restaurant to run. I know you have things to do too; people to see . . ." She stopped painfully, thinking, *And places to go.* Oh, yes. He was definitely going places.

They shared a tortured look. He shook his head. "Betty—"

"Please don't. I'll come by the wedding parlor tonight. Don't say anything else right now."

He swallowed roughly, his expression harsh with re-

straint, and nodded. "I'm going over to the sheriff's office and borrow a car."

"Take the Mercedes instead. I have my van out back."

"Mercedes aren't my style, babe." He kissed her slowly. His eyes shut, he tilted his forehead against hers for a moment. "See you later."

She watched him leave, then dropped into a chair. The future was now the present. It was empty.

The couple, Max's last wedding for the night, appeared to be in their mid-twenties. She was a plump little sugar cookie with frightened eyes. He had the swagger of a Saturday-night hell-raiser but the smile of a shy Boy Scout. They'd inquired about a costume package, but had hastily declined when Norma mentioned that the costume weddings started at $59.95.

They stepped slowly and awkwardly up the aisle toward Max, trying to keep time with the ponderous wedding march that boomed from Norma's organ. The groom wore a mud-brown polyester suit. The bride wore a dress of pink ruffles that emphasized every extra snack she'd ever eaten. They held hands and stared at Max fixedly. He could almost hear their knees knocking in duet.

When Max glanced at Norma, she cut her eyes at the couple and shook her head. Doomed from the start, she was saying.

He silently agreed. But what the hell? He'd married lots of pairs who had looked this hopeless. The unhappiness they were contemplating wasn't his problem. He had enough unhappiness to contemplate himself.

Max smoothed the long coat of his black marrying outfit, then clasped his hands in front of himself in his solemn marrying pose, the right hand cupped over the bulky mitten of bandages that covered the left. He was ready to begin his spiel. He forced himself to stop thinking about Betty.

Betty didn't cooperate. One of the double doors opened

at the back of the room. She slipped inside, dressed in new sneakers, new jeans, a T-shirt, and a gray sweater, with her hair pulled back in a haphazard ponytail. She looked tired and bedraggled. He wanted to forget everything else and carry her off to their rented room.

She met his eyes with a fathomless gaze as she sat down in the back row. Aside from himself and Norma she was the couple's only audience. Max tried to hide his anger. This was a pathetic atmosphere for a wedding. Where was the reverence, the joy, the excitement?

The back doors opened again. Audubon stepped into the room, looked around with amusement, then nodded to Betty—who straightened ominously. Audubon flicked an invisible bit of lint from the aviator's jacket he wore with black trousers and a white sweater. He sat down across the aisle from Betty and glanced from her to Max with the hint of a frown.

Max cursed silently. Audubon hadn't bothered to return the phone call; he'd flown down from Virginia to pursue a deal in person. He probably had an employment contract out in his limo, ready for Max's signature. He didn't take chances when he sensed victory close at hand.

Norma hit the last notes of the wedding march. The couple stopped abruptly, bumping against each other, still clenching each other's hands. Max cleared his throat. He looked at the scrubbed, frightened faces of the young man and woman, who waited for his usual, meaningless crap about matrimony. He couldn't make himself say it.

"Why are you here?" he demanded bluntly, scowling at them.

They jumped in unison. The groom turned red with embarrassment. "You think we shouldn't be here, huh?"

"I don't know. Why are you getting married?"

The bride began to sputter. "B-because we l-love each other—"

"That's not enough," Max told her. "You have to love each other in a certain way. You have to be willing to

love each other even when one of you is impossible to love. You have to be willing to take the other person's pain as if it were your own. You have to want the other person's happiness as much—if not more—than you want your own happiness."

"We've got all that," the groom said defensively.

"Tell me something. You two look like you haven't got an extra dime between you. Is that any way to start a marriage? Have you got any place to live? Do you have decent jobs?"

"Stop it, Max," Betty said brokenly. The couple swiveled around and stared at her. She stood up and looked at Max with tears in her eyes. Then she looked at the couple. "It doesn't matter if you don't have very much money, or a wonderful place to live, or decent jobs. If you really want to take care of each other for the rest of your lives, you can build a good life together."

"I work at the gas station over on highway seven," the groom told her. "And I just bought a double-wide trailer."

Max shook his head. "But what if you lose your job? How will you make the trailer payments?"

"I'd get another job!"

The bride pivoted toward him and lifted her chin. "I can pay 'em. I work days at the Hamburger Barn and nights at the Laundromat."

Betty applauded. "You two are going to be just fine."

Max met her angry, sad gaze and held it firmly. He felt as if he were strangling inside. *Take the last step. It's such a small one. See if she believes in your newfound faith.* "What if he wants to give her more than he's capable of giving, and it makes him do things that hurt her?" Max asked.

The anger faded from her expression. "Are we still talking about money, or are we talking about loyalty, commitment, and promises built on faith?"

"We're talking about money. The rest—he can give that, all of it, because he knows he'll never stop loving her. She's changed his attitude toward making prom-

ises, you see. But maybe he's worried that she won't believe him, because he's been so stubborn and confused in the past."

Her hands rose slowly to her mouth. "Maybe she trusts the future more than the past. Maybe she trusts him in a way that she's never trusted anyone else, because he's always been honest about his feelings."

The bride and groom looked at each other in bewilderment. "Huh?" the groom said.

At the back of the room Audubon leaned on the back of a chair, his chin propped on one hand. He looked disgruntled. "Sssh, children. We're merely spectators."

Max continued to hold Betty's gaze. "He hasn't always been honest. He let her think that he wanted to make money more than he wanted to stay with her. He thought the money would make her believe in him more."

She moved slowly into the aisle, never looking away from him, her hands still raised to her lips in amazement. "He thought she'd be uncertain about his motives?"

Max nodded. "Would you say that he's wrong?"

"Without a doubt." She glided toward him as if floating on forces that didn't require her conscious will. "Do you think he'll stay with her?"

"Without a doubt." Max stepped down from the platform. He held out his good hand. "Do you think she'll believe him when he says he can look into the future and see himself as a husband and father?"

"Oh, she wants to believe that most of all."

He met her halfway up the aisle. She took his hand and stepped closer to him. With the space of a whisper between them Max asked, "Do you think she'll marry him?"

Her eyes glistened. She lifted his hand to her lips and kissed it. "At the very first opportunity."

He pulled her into his arms and tucked her head against the crook of his neck. "Then they should definitely get married."

The bride and groom stared at him hopefully. "Us too?"

"You too. But I tell you what. Go change into the costumes you wanted. This marriage ceremony is going to be the best I've ever performed. And it's on the house."

He sighed happily as Betty began laughing and kissed his cheek. Norma whooped. Audubon stood with great dignity. A rueful smile touched his mouth. "I suppose," he said dryly, "that I'm not surprised."

Holding each other deep in the heart of the night, they finally gave up. Each time they tried to be solemn and discuss the future, they were distracted by the present, and made love again.

"We don't have a place to live," he reminded her.

"And very little to wear in public."

"Not to mention only one toothbrush. Did you have to buy a pink one?"

"We'll pool our resources and get you a blue one."

"Okay. I'm happy."

"You feel happy. Very happy. Oh, Maximilian—"

"Now, stop doing that. Yes, keep your hands right there, and be still. Be serious. What kind of wedding do you want?"

"Why don't we have a military wedding? I'd love to see you in uniform. We could invite the men from your old team."

"I'd like that," he answered gruffly. "It'll be dignified, I promise you. I won't treat it like one of the parlor weddings. It's not a joke to me."

She kissed him. "But you can't let me be dull and stuffy, Major."

"Well, you could wear the Daisy Mae outfit."

They both laughed. "I think not," she told him. "Perhaps I'll just let Faux Paw be my bridesmaid. That should liven things up."

"I can't wait to see *that*. We should do it soon."

"I'd love to."

"Love me?"

"Forever."

Now he was the one who couldn't keep from distracting them from conversation. Betty sighed happily as he began touching her. The man could do such amazing things with only one good hand.

"I look forward to a lot more attention like this," she whispered.

"I guarantee you'll have it. Along with a lot of love."

She traced his lips with her fingertips, anticipating his smile before she felt it. So much hard work lay ahead of them. So much to rebuild. So many risks to take. She and Max should stop being irresponsible and become properly depressed.

No way. She kissed him, moved closer, and knew that the future was safe and happy within her arms.

THE EDITOR'S CORNER

This summer Bantam has not only provided you with a mouth-watering lineup of LOVESWEPTs, but with some excellent women's fiction as well. We wanted to alert you to several terrific books which are available right now from your bookseller.

A few years ago we published a unique, sophisticated love story in the LOVESWEPT line called **AZURE DAYS, QUICKSILVER NIGHTS** by talented author Carole Nelson Douglas. Carole has an incredible imagination, and her idea for her next project just knocked our socks off. Set in Las Vegas, **CRYSTAL DAYS**—a June release—and **CRYSTAL NIGHTS**—a July release—are delightfully entertaining books. Each features two love stories and the crazy character Midnight Louie, who can't be described in mere words. Don't miss these two summer treats.

Speaking of treats, Nora Roberts's long-awaited next book, **PUBLIC SECRETS,** is on the stands! Nora's strengths as a writer couldn't be showcased better than in this riveting novel of romantic suspense. **PUBLIC SECRETS** is summer reading at its very best!

Now, on to the LOVESWEPTs we have in store for you!

Suzanne Forster writes with powerful style about characters who are larger than life. In **THE DEVIL AND MS. MOODY,** LOVESWEPT #414, you'll meet two such characters. Edwina Moody, hot on the trail of a missing heir to a fortune, finds her destiny in the arms of an irresistible rebel named Diablo. Edwina is more than out of her element among a bunch of rough-and-tumble bikers, yet Diablo makes her feel as if she's finally found home. On his own mission, Diablo sees a chance to further both their causes, and he convinces Edwina to make a bargain with the devil himself. You'll soon discover—along with Edwina—that Diablo is somewhat a sheep in wolf's clothing, as he surrenders his heart to the woman who longs to possess him. Much of the impact of this wonderful love story is conveyed through Suzanne's writing. I guarantee you'll want to savor every word!

This month several of our characters find themselves in some pretty desperate situations. In **RELENTLESS,** LOVESWEPT #415 by Patt Bucheister, heroine Dionne Hart takes over the helm of a great business empire—and comes face-to-face once again with the man she'd loved fifteen years

(continued)

before. Nick Lyon remembers the blushing teenager with the stormy eyes, and is captivated by the elegant woman she's become. He's relentless in his pursuit of Dionne, but she can't bring herself to share her secrets with a man she had loved but never trusted, a writer who couldn't do his job and respect her privacy too. But Nick won't take no for an answer and continues to knock down the walls of her resistance until all she can do is give in to her desire. Patt will have you rooting loudly for these two people and for their happiness. If only men like Nick could be cloned!

Talk about a desperate situation! Terry Lawrence certainly puts Cally Baldwin in one in **WANTED: THE PERFECT MAN,** LOVESWEPT #416. What would you do if you'd just dumped the latest in a long line of losers and had made a vow to swear off men—then met a man your heart told you was definitely *the one*! Cally does the logical thing, she decides to be "just friends" with Steve Rousseau. But Cally isn't fooling anyone with her ploy—and Steve knows her sizzling good-night kisses are his proof. He takes his time in wooing her, cultivating her trust and faith in him. Much to his dismay, however, he realizes Cally has more than just a few broken relationships in her past to overcome before he can make her believe in forever. And just when he thinks she's lost him, Cally learns Steve really is her perfect man. All you readers who've yet to find someone who fits your personal wanted poster's description will take heart after reading this lively romance. And those of you who have the perfect man will probably think of a few more qualities to add to his list.

If you've been following the exploits of the group of college friends Tami Hoag introduced in her *Rainbow Chasers* series, you're no doubt awaiting Jayne Jordan's love story. in **REILLY'S RETURN,** LOVESWEPT #417, Jayne finds the answer her heart and soul have been seeking. Since Jayne is quite a special lady, no ordinary man could dream of winning her. It takes the likes of Pat Reilly, the Australian movie star the press has dubbed the Hunk from Down Under, to disturb Jayne's inner peace. As much as she'd like to deny it, all the signs point to the fact that Reilly is her destiny—but that doesn't make the journey into forever with him any less tempestuous. Tami has an innate ability to mix humor with tender sensuality, creating the kind of story you tell us you love so much—one that can make you laugh and
(continued)

make you cry. Don't pass up the opportunity to experience a truly memorable love story in **REILLY'S RETURN.**

At last Joan Elliott Pickart has answered your requests and written Dr. Preston Harper's story! Joan has received more mail about Preston Harper over the years than about any other character, so she wanted to take extra care to give him a special lady love and story all his own. With **PRESTON HARPER, M.D.,** LOVESWEPT #418, Joan fulfills every expectation. As a pediatrician, Preston's love for children is his life's calling, but he longs to be a real dad. The problem is, he doesn't see himself in the role of husband! When Dinah Bradshaw walks into his office with the child who's made her an instant mom, Preston's well-ordered plans suddenly fall flat. But Dinah doesn't want marriage any more than Preston had—she's got a law career to get off the ground. Can you guess what happens to these two careful people when love works its magic on them?

Next in her *SwanSea Place* series is Fayrene Preston's **THE PROMISE,** LOVESWEPT #419. In this powerful story of an impossible love Fayrene keeps you on the edge of your seat, breathless with anticipation as Conall Deverell honors a family promise to Sharon Graham—a promise to make her pregnant! Sharon vows she wants nothing else from the formidable man who'd broken her heart ten years before by claiming that the child she'd carried wasn't his. But neither can control the passion that flares between them as Sharon accepts Conall's challenge to make him want her, make his blood boil. You've come to expect the ultimate in a romance from Fayrene, and she doesn't disappoint with **THE PROMISE!**

Best wishes from the entire LOVESWEPT staff,
Sincerely,

Susann Brailey

Susann Brailey
Editor
LOVESWEPT
Bantam Books
666 Fifth Avenue
New York, NY 10103

Mary Gregg

Reading has always been a part of my life. I come from a long line of readers who consider books treasured friends. I cannot imagine a life without books—how dull and bland it would be.

LOVESWEPTs are *the best* contemporary romances due to one lady, Carolyn Nichols. From the beginning Carolyn promised quality not quantity, and she has kept her promise over the years.

Some of my favorite authors are: Sandra Brown—she must use her husband as a hero model; Kay Hooper, who I can always depend on for her wonderful sense of humor; Iris Johansen; Helen Mittermeyer; Linda Cajio; Billie Green; Joan Elliott Pickart; and Fayrene Preston, who reminds me a little of Shirley Temple.

At the end of the day I can curl up with a LOVESWEPT and transport myself back to the days of my childhood, when Prince Charming and Cinderella were my friends. After all, romance stories are modern fairy tales for grown-ups, in which the characters live happily ever after.